Preview

Heading down the hallway to the poetry workshop, I glanced back and spotted Curtis a few feet behind. He motioned for me to come to him. I stopped in my tracks and waited for him to catch up.

"How you doing?" Curtis greeted.

"I'm fine."

"I know that. Tell me something I don't know," he gave me a warm hug.

The mere touch of his hand sent a warming shiver through me. I savored the moment in my mind. "So how are you?" I asked.

"Oh I'm phenomenal," he smiled.

His smile made me feel so happy inside. I managed a tentative smile in return. I could sense a connection, a kindling deep within. Curtis and I walked into the class together as if we were a couple. We sat next to each other.

Ms. Sinclair wrote notes on the board. "There's a poetry form that originated in India, called the Naani. It consists of 4 lines. The total lines contain 20 to 25 syllables. The following is an example of a Naani."

> Romantic love is
> looking for me.
> Around some winding
> road we'll find each other.

After I wrote a Naani, I knew that poetry would remain an important part of my life, long after the workshop.

> Love was a mysterious
> stranger, who became
> my closest friend,
> since I've known you.

"Have you written one?" Curtis asked.

"Yes," I replied.

"Show me yours and I'll show you mines," he smiled.

We traded journals.

> Love's anatomy
> between you and me.
> I'm loving your face your mind.
> If you want me show me a sign.

After I read the poem, somehow I knew that Curtis had addressed it to me. He was letting me know in no subtle way, that I had attracted his attention. He's looking at me with so much interest. He's nibbling on my bait. Now, all I have to do is catch him.

"Nicely done. Your Naani reminds me of a note from the inside of a greeting card. I like it," Curtis told me as he handed my journal back to me.

"Thank you. I like your poetry too. I'm into the anatomy of love," I smiled at him.

"Poetry is so intimate. It's filled with feelings," he told me.

"Yes it is," I replied as I handed him his journal.

"I'm glad I'm getting to know you better," his gaze met mines.

"Same here," I smiled into his eyes.

It seems I was getting close to Curtis through poetry. I loved being able to see him more than once a week. I wanted to find out more about him. I couldn't help wondering what sort of person he was, where he was from, where he lives, what he eats, his likes and dislikes. I'd like to discover the real person beneath his superstar image . . . . He seemed decent enough, if I were any judge of character.

A pupil raised her hand.

Ms. Sinclair nodded.

"My name is Pratiti and I have a Naani to share. I'm Asian Indian. Thank you for teaching us about a poetry form that's from my native land. Here's my Naani . . ."

> Paper faces,
> thinking one thing,
> saying another, hiding
> what's beneath the surface.

"Very interesting Naani," Ms. Sinclair clapped.

The class applauded.

"Anyone else?" the instructor scanned the room.

A few other students recited their poems.

Analyzing my feelings for Curtis, I came to the conclusion that it was more than infatuation. I've admired him in the past. But now my affection for him had somehow deepened.

I wished Curtis were mine, and then I felt guilty for wanting a man who's engaged to be married. A thought of Curtis making love to Crystal flashed through the corridors of my mind and I became nauseous. I looked over at Curtis with wishful eyes, and for a moment his face reminded me of an angel. My whole being seemed filled with waiting. "Oh God, I think I love him," I whispered to myself.

FINDING MY GRAVY

Joyce Gantt

Order this book online at www.trafford.com
or email orders@trafford.com
Most Trafford titles are also available at major online book retailers.

Library of Congress Cataloging-in-Publication Data

Finding My Gravy / Joyce Gantt. -First Edition.

ISBN: 978-1-4669-0251-0 (sc)
ISBN: 978-1-4669-0252-7 (hc)
ISBN: 978-1-4669-0253-4 (e)

Library of Congress Control Number: 2011919600

1. Fiction / Romance / General. 2. Love.
3. Dating (Social customs) 4. Race relations / Fiction.
I. Title.

Trafford rev. 11/10/2011

 www.trafford.com

North America & international
toll-free: 1 888 232 4444 (USA & Canada)
phone: 250 383 6864 ♦ fax: 812 355 4082

Joyce Gantt

Joyce was born and raised in southern California. She loves to express herself through novel writing. She attended Pierce College and studied music and other elements of the arts. She also enjoys singing, playing her guitar, writing music and poetry. She strives to make art and culture an ongoing part of her life. Joyce now resides in Alabama, near the Gulf Coast area.

Dedication

I dedicate this book to those who desire a true
love who is faithful as a homing pigeon.
May you have a love that is patient, kind and enduring.

Chapter 1

I suppose most women dream of finding their gravy, someday. Gravy, is another word I use for man of my dreams. My definition of gra·vy: man who will make my life deliciously complete. Like sauce on rice, gravy enhances what's already good. Oh yes, I want my gravy right now.

It all began in the summer of 2010, my love strings were finally stroked. I had been romantically shy, but now I see things differently.

Let me take you on a rhapsodic trip. Believe me, it can happen, because it happened to me.

Pressing the down button the elevator doors opened on the fifth-floor, crowded with people. Attempting to step inside, I managed to squeeze in. The high-pitched ring of my cell phone sounded, which added more pain to my pulsing headache. Scrambling around in my purse, I retrieved the phone expeditiously.

"Hello," I frowned. Kneading my throbbing temple, I wished the pain would subside.

"Oh hi Joi. Happy Friday!" Tiffany's voice chimed.

"Thank goodness it's Friday," I sighed.

"You sound a little down. What's wrong?" she asked.

"Today was bananas, and I'm still stressed out about it. Oh, my head is aching," I moaned.

"Ah, poor Joi. Why do you have to have an headache now?" she whined. "Damn, I wanted us to go clubbing tonight."

"How about a rain check on our girls night out?"

"Tell you what, go home, get refreshed, and take something for that damn headache. Feel better, so we can go," she demanded.

"I don't know Tiffany," I replied. Heading out the Health Gist National upscale corporate office building, I exited the elevator and walked down the plush burgundy-carpeted floor through the main lobby.

"Ah, come on. Stop isolating yourself. It would do you some good to get out and take off some of the edge. You know what they say about all work and no play."

"No. What do they say about it?" I joked as I walked out the transparent glass double doors.

A laugh skipped through my phone. "Joi, shut up."

Glancing up at the warm sunshine sparkling through the leaves of the trees, I headed for the parking lot to my silver 2007 BMW. "I'll see how I feel later. I'll give you a ring."

"Alright. Feel better."

"Thanks. Bye." I jumped into my car and headed back to my multicolored brick house in Valley Village, California. I could hardly wait to take a pain reliever and unwind from my irksome workday.

The pain reliever I swallowed earlier worked a wonder. I actually felt well enough to go out that evening.

Club Improvise had a talented group perform that night. The soulful live music made me feel like dancing, but my shyness wouldn't allow me to let loose on the dance floor.

Scanning the interior design of the nightclub, I noticed that the ceiling had an awesome array of stars, like a midnight sky. "The posh decor of this place is so awakening, with all the brilliant colors. This is a nice one," I nodded.

"Pelar, the owner, is definitely a romantic," Tiffany looked up.

The waiter returned to our table with some drinks and delectable appetizers.

"Thank you," I told him.

"You're very welcome," he replied.

Feeling like a spectator, I glanced to my left, my right, and then I looked straight ahead. I spotted an intriguingly handsome guy, busting a smooth move on the dance floor as I was sipping my drink. He seemed as if he was enjoying himself. My eyes glanced over the modest black dress and the classical-styled white pumps I had on. While I checked my lipstick in my silver compact mirror, I tried to release my inhibitions. "I'm heading for that one, right there," I told Tiffany.

"Go for it," she smiled.

Taking a deep breath, I stood up from my seat and started towards him. Suddenly, this redhead swooped in and wisped away with the dreamy sought after prey. She had the nerve to eye me as they danced across the floor. I slowly retraced my steps back to my seat.

"You have to be quick," Tiffany told me.

"Ah crap. Did you see what that trifling trick did? She knew I was headed for him," I huffed.

Sipping her drink, Tiffany nodded.

Nibbling on some appetizers, I sulked silently.

The performer announced that the dance floor was open as she sang an upbeat tune.

Tiffany strutted with confidence to the dance floor in her purple-print dress, and danced alluringly. She shook her hips about, and bopped her head from side to side. Her blond curls bounced with finesse. Then, with a smile on her quaint face, she darted her green eyes over at the guy she wanted to dance with, and he came to her like a piece of steel drawn to a magnet.

Tiffany and I had been best friends for nearly two years. She was the kind of white girl who liked snagging well-to-do, fine black men.

While I sat alone at the table that evening, I realized that I needed to make a major adjustment in my personality, or I could remain single indefinitely. I wished I were more outgoing towards the opposite-sex, like Tiffany. I had been reserved and work absorbed, but I didn't want to be that way anymore. Being that I was raised conservative, I didn't have free and easy ways.

Guys used to always show interest in me, but I never gave them a chance. Since I had played hard to get for so long, I felt stuck in reverse. I was having a heck of a time trying to switch my gear into drive. I need to stop being shy and go on a manhunt, I thought. So, here I am in solo-fashion. I'm ready for love, but must I compromise my views to snag a man? Must good girls finish last? I'll see.

Out of all my friends, I think Destiny is the most eccentric. She's a mystical Piscean, who's proud to be biracial. She's into affirmations, attracting positive energy and eliminating the negative. There must be something to it, because Destiny is such a pleasant person to be around. She introduced me to aromatherapy.

"I brought you a house warming gift," Destiny smiled as she handed me a floral gift bag. "I know you've been here for a few months now, but better late than never."

"Thank you Miss Destiny," I said as I looked inside the bag.

"It's an essential oil. Lemon uplifts you emotionally, mentally and spiritually. What you do is, put a few quick dabs onto your wrist and it'll boost your mood and uplift your spirit. Whenever I'm in a bit of a funk, lemon always works for me. The feather is to bring you calm."

"How can a feather bring calm?" I asked.

"The energies from the feathers of a gentle bird, brings calm. You place it under your pillow for a more restful sleep."

"Oh," I said. I honestly didn't know whether to believe that or not.

"What's for dinner?" she asked.

"I have a healthy frozen pizza in the fridge. I bought it from Health Way Grocers. The pizzas they carry actually taste very good."

"I sure do like their cream cheese carrot cookies."

We walked into my kitchen. Destiny removed a frozen cheesecake and some green grapes out of a bag and placed the items on the counter. "I brought desert," she cheerfully said. "I also brought a new movie I'd like for you to see. We can watch it after we eat."

Removing the pizza out of the fridge, I placed it on a cooking pan and shoved it in the oven.

"So what have you been up to?" she asked as she took plates down from the kitchen cabinet.

"I've been thinking about finding love. I signed up with an Internet dating service called Dream Match. I suppose I'll see how that pans out," I answered while I rinsed the grapes off over the sink.

"To find the right man, you must get in tune with the microcosm of life. Being that you're a Scorpio you should stay away from a Leo," Destiny advised.

"Now you're confusing me," I sighed. "I know you mean well, but I think I would be better off following my gut feeling about a man."

"I'm an intellectual twenty-eight year old, who knows the signs. I repeat, no Leos," she warned.

"Whatever," I shrugged my shoulders.

I've been a discreet woman, whose life revolved around my job. I've redundantly gone to work and returned back home. I've rarely hung out, except for times I've tagged along with a friend to a club.

At times my work seems monotonous to me. Here, I feel like a fixture, like a picture on the wall.

Some of my coworkers are friendly some are not. Lately, I've been thinking this is not where I belong. I'm staying for now because the pay is good and I feel needed. I do have a nice panoramic view from my office window. I can see the rustic mountains from here.

"The elevator broke down; that's why I'm late," Marshall explained as he stood in the doorway of my office.

"Does the Maintenance Department know about the elevator?" I asked.

"I used the emergency phone that was located inside the elevator and they got me out," he breathed heavily.

"Drink some water or something. Go get refreshed. I'll adjust your time in," I told him.

"Thanks. I need a drink," he said.

"No happy-juice allowed," I told him lightheartedly.

He laughed and left my office.

Pushing back from my solid oak desk, I stood up from my brown leather swivel chair. To make sure things were running smoothly in my department, I left my office to walk the floor of the call center for a while.

It's against company rules for me to be romantically involved with any associate who is under my supervision. If that were not the case, I'd definitely like to go out with Marshall. He seems like a decent-enough guy. I'm in a better mood from just looking at him. He's easy on the eyes. I think he sort of likes me too; I can tell by the way he looks at me. Forbidden fruit can be so tempting.

There are two other guys I get along with who are not off-limits, but I've never socialized with either of them outside of work. Go figure, on that one.

"I must get my mind on my work," I scolded myself. I'm so far behind on my quality assurance reports, I thought as I headed back to my office.

"Mmm, the food smells so good," I inhaled the savory aroma of the mouthwatering dish as I pulled up a chair to the dinner table.

"It is good. Help yourself," my Momma motioned towards the tender king salmon, the spicy string beans and the delicious potato salad.

Rubbing my hands together, I quickly selected satisfying portions for myself. There's nothing like Mom's home cooking. "Yum," I chewed a bite. "Could you pass me the hot sauce please?"

"There you go," she shook some hot sauce on my salmon.

"The salmon tastes so fresh; it's very delicious. The string beans have a kick to 'em," I swallowed.

"The doctor's report said that your Dad's blood pressure is too high, so I've been trying out other spices to wean him off of using so much salt, but it's not working," she shook her head. "I'm glad you like it."

"Daddy needs to stop taking everything so lightly," I voiced with concern.

"He won't listen to me. I'm worried about him," she sighed.

"I'll have a talk with him."

"Why are you two talking about me so?" He walked in the chandeliered dining room towards the dinner table chuckling as if he didn't have a care in the world.

"Daddy, you need to stop consuming so much salt and drink more water to get your blood pressure down!" I advised in an amplified voice.

"Woo, don't talk to me so loud. I can hear ya!" he exclaimed. He took a seat at the table. "So how's my Joi doing?" he gave me a gentle smile.

"I'm doing okay. Mom and I are concerned about you," I firmly stated as I eyed him.

"I'll do better bay. Just give me time," he gave me a pat on the back.

"You need to lessen your salt intake right away," I insisted.

"If I get my pressure down, will you get married and give me some grandchildren?" he smirked and took a huge bite of food.

"I have to find my Mr. Right first."

"Randy Kennedy, an eligible businessman, inquired about you," Momma smiled at me.

"Who?" My eyebrows rose out of curiosity.

"His Father recently made him the new owner of Kennedy Construction. Your Dad and I have done business with his Father in the past. Well anyway, while I was at the market the other day I saw him there. I struck up a conversation with Randy and told him about you. After I showed him your picture he seemed interested, so I gave him your phone number," she beamed with hope.

"Ah Ma, why did you have to give him my phone number?" I complained.

"Joi, you're thirty-eight years old. You're single with no prospects. Your Mother thought that maybe you needed a little help," he defended Ma's actions.

"Don't worry about me, okay. I'll get a man," I stated with optimism.

"We don't want you to wait too late, is all," he added.

"I'm not going to wait too late. I'm honestly looking right now," I exasperated.

"Let me give you a tip. A good man likes a woman who has a life. It would be great for you to have an interest in something else other than work. You need to become more interesting, so a man will look your way for more than your looks. Maybe you can take up a hobby or skill and use it for a conversation piece. That's the way to become a keeper," Mother advised.

Absorbed in my Momma's words, I thought out loud, "I've always wanted to play the flute."

"There you go," he supported. "Thanks for trying to help her sweets," Dad winked at Momma.

"Well she's a Glamier. Glamiers are never unlucky at love," she spooned a bite.

"Love seekers know they'll find some good lovin' with us," he grinned.

"You're right about that," she rubbed Dad's thigh.

"Get a room," I smirked.

"As soon as you leave we will," Dad remarked.

They giggled.

Oh geez, now I'm being pressured to live up to the family's reputation of being lucky at love, when I've never even touched first base, I squirmed inside my mind.

"Joi, a woman who looks like you usually knows how to use what she's got. You're letting your beauty go to waste wearing those boring cloths," Tiffany tugged on the sleeve of my navy businesslike blouse. "You could snag just about any guy if you tried."

"My wardrobe does need a makeover," I admitted.

"Well, let's go to my favorite place to shop, Allures Edge."

"I'd like to buy something a little sexy." I smiled glancing at the shopping centers as we walked through the crowded Glendale Mall.

"If you really want a man, you must awaken the cougar within you. You need to become aggressive."

"How do I go from being shy to aggressive?" I asked as we stepped onto the escalator that was going upwards to the second floor.

"Wear brighter colors, to have a bolder mood," she replied in an as a matter of fact tone of voice.

"I'll buy something red then," I smiled to myself. "I'm going to completely change my style. I've decided I need to look more . . . interesting," I told Tiffany.

"Well it's about time," she cut her eyes at me as we stepped off the escalator.

"Hey beautiful!" a guy shouted out as he walked over to us.

"That's Max, the guy I hit-it-off with at the club. He's so hot," Tiffany squeaked with excitement.

"What's up baby?" he gave her a hug.

"I'm just hanging out shopping with my best friend. Max meet Joi," she introduced.

"Hi," I offered a hand.

"Girl, move your hand. I give hugs," he squeezed me in a tight embrace. "Oh," he moaned.

"You're such a flirt," I eyed him.

"That's just Max being Max," she said.

"Yeah, I'm really friendly," he grinned.

"Max and I have a date tonight," she broadcast. "How cool is that?"

I didn't know what to think about Max.

"Your friend is so quiet," he eyed me.

"Pick me up at eight and don't be late," she smiled at him.

"Sure thing babe. I've gotta go. See you around," Max stared at me as he stepped away into the crowd.

He was attractive and unscrupulous enough to take any woman.

"Well, what do you think about him?"

"He's dangerously flirtatious," I warned her.

"Like I said, that's Max being Max." Tiffany led the way into Allure's Edge.

"Let's shop," I searched the racks.

"Look at this," she fingered an outfit.

"That's not what I'm looking for," I snubbed.

"What then?"

"Oh now, here are some possibilities," I smiled over the garment rack at Tiffany. Pulling some clothing from the rack, I held up a red frock in front of me as I gazed in the mirror.

"I wish I saw that first. Let's see how it looks on you. Try it on," she urged.

Rushing into the dressing room, I stepped out a moment later modeling the sexy red dress. "Oou, this is so me," I pranced in front of the mirror.

"That's a must have for you," she told me.

Nodding, I felt a beam of happiness flash through me. "This dress makes me feel confident," I held my head up.

"Guess what?" Tiffany held something in back of her.

"What?" I replied.

"I'm buying this to wear on my date tonight," she showed me an orange translucent revealing frock.

"You're a bad girl. That's way over the top even for you," I voiced in shock.

"This dress will give me the guarantee that Max will only have eyes for me tonight."

"Max is a good looking black man, but he's kind of strayish. Is there any other reason why you like him?" I questioned curiously.

"Girl did you see the size of Max's hands? If you don't know what that means you're way too green."

"You're nasty," I whispered to her.

"I always use condoms so it's not that nasty."

"Oh yes it is," I debated.

"You're right. It is," she laughed aloud.

"You need to start coming to church."

"I'll think about it."

"Oou I like those stilettos. I'm going to buy a pair in red," I searched for my size.

"Those are hot."

"So what do you think of my selections?" I asked.

"It's totally not your style, but you needed a change."

"Well, here goes the new me," I looked in the mirror.

I hope that my attempt to change my personality from shy to outgoing towards the opposite-sex will be a success. I suppose I could pretend I'm not shy. That's it. I'll fake it, till I make it, I thought as I headed to the checkout counter.

Since I've aged gracefully, I haven't thought much about my age till lately. I find myself thinking how time has flown by.

I went online to check the Dream Match Website for potential love matches. Well, most of the so-called love matches my age or older looked like crap. Evidently they must not have taken good care of themselves. About one or two of them looked passable, but I didn't like their profiles. I actually have the nerve to be picky at my age. I would like to have a good man in my life though. Maybe I'll compromise on some things to get a good one.

I'm not like those other well-to-do women of color who say they don't need a man. I admit I need a man. Just because a woman can take care of herself, doesn't mean she has to do this thing called life alone. Money can't keep her company. I imagine those fake dildos won't satisfy forever.

Even though I'm this incredibly great individual with no baggage, I'm still single. I'm determined to not remain an onlooker when it comes to having a true love.

I must make up a foolproof plan to win and keep Mr. Right, I thought as I picked up a pencil and note pad and began to write . . .

Step 1: I must stop being shy or fake it till I make it.

The next step in my plan to land a man is to take Mom's advice and have an interest in something else other than work. I need to become more interesting. Now I have a personal drive. Step 2: Flute lessons here I come.

To become more attractive to men I've updated my wardrobe. Step 3: I've traded in my nerd garb for a more interesting sexier look.

Chapter 2

Health Gist National held an offsite town hall meeting at the Oasis Tavern that afternoon. It was a lovely Indian summer type of day. While I was on the way there, the bumper-to-bumper traffic slowed down to a crawl, because of other associates driving to the same meeting. I parked my car in the designated area and headed for the hotel's large conference room. I walked inside and quickly found a seat.

Several speakers from various Health Gist National locations shared that day.

A stout man with red curly hair, dressed business casual, walked up to the microphone.

"Hello, my name is Mr. Langston. For those of you who are new to Health Gist National, I'm the CEO of this great corporation. I need not remind you that we have had a great second quarter this year. We've beat some of our competitor's bids and gained new employer groups," he reflected.

We hooted.

"We are a team; links in a chain. A chain is only as strong as its weakest link. Weak customer service makes a weak business. Together we can reach our goal of becoming the number one health insurance company, nationally. The way for us to become number one is by providing our members with excellent customer service. People are you with me?" he asked.

"Yes," I cheered along with the other associates.

"In every relationship, business or romantic, you have to show commitment to build trust and loyalty. We all want to be treated with courtesy and respect. Let's provide prompt solutions to our member's inquiries, so we will remain their choice. Let's give our members what they want and they'll stay with us. Am I right?"

"Yes," we shouted.

In my opinion, Mr. Langston was the most memorable speaker there. I thought he was very candid about ways to make Health Gist National more efficient.

"Hey Joi," Gege greeted as she rolled her shopping cart in my direction.

"Oh hi Gege," I waved and continued looking at the various brands of hair relaxers on the shelves.

"Girl, get away from those hair relaxers. You don't need a perm," she frowned.

"I'm ready for a new look," I told her.

"Suit yourself. If I had pretty hair like yours, I would've never had my hair relaxed."

"You always have your hair looking fine and fresh. Gege, which brand of relaxer would be best for my type of hair?"

She touched a few strands of my hair. "Since your hair is soft and wavy, a kidee perm would be best. Kidee perms are more milder." She gazed at my head of dark flowing hair, "Joi, don't mess up your good hair."

Leaning down, I picked up a box of hair relaxer from off the shelf and placed it in my shopping cart. "I'll give it some more thought," I shrugged.

"Once it's done you can't undo it," she warned.

"If I decide to use it and I don't like it, I'll just let the perm grow out."

"I see you're just as stubborn as ever."

"Hey, I resent that remark," I giggled.

"If the shoe fits then wear it," she snapped.

"I haven't even made up my mind yet. Moving on. I heard that you and Brent are going to get married. When is the big day?" I inquired with excitement in my voice.

Gege's mouth grew tight and grim. "He wasn't the man I thought he was," she managed to reply through stiff lips.

"I'm sorry it didn't work out for you. What happened?" I asked out of curiosity.

"It's too painful for me to speak of," a tear rolled down her cheek. "Brent kept a lot of secrets. That asshole was not like he seemed," she sniffled.

"I didn't mean to be intrusive. It's just that I'm trying to find love and I . . ."

"Then I suggest that you look deep before you leap," she sighed.

"Yeah," I nodded.

"I'll call you whenever I feel ready to talk about it," she muttered.

"Here's my current phone number," I scribbled my telephone number down on a piece of paper.

"Alright," she nodded.

It was a surprise to hear that Gege and Brent's relationship hadn't worked out. Those two seemed so good together. I wondered what happened.

I love myself, so I try not to put myself in situations that I may later regret. Finding the right man can be tricky, but I think I'm intuitive enough to do it.

Nowadays, some people are so casual about sex as if it's like shaking someone's hand. Life-threatening sexually transmittable diseases are at epidemic proportions, and it seems like a lot of people just don't care anymore. I find that strange. They're trying to ignore the danger that's obviously there. What's going on? All I know is I need to live life differently.

I love myself so that I may know how to love others. I don't need to be too shy neither too eager around a potential love interest. I need to find balance in my life.

Some people say that love is the answer, but if that's true, why are there so many broken hearts in the world? A man once said, "Love, like your heart has never been broken." If my heart had been broken, I'd find that hard to do.

I'm so careful about who I open up to. I mean there are some people who belong in a person's sphere of life and there are some who don't belong. I'm waiting for the day when I feel it's okay to let my guard down. Having background checks done are not just good for employers. I suppose love is all about taking chances. When you love someone, you stand a chance of being rejected. Some may even see love as a weakness, but true love is what brings beauty to life.

This game call love can be like attempting to win the lottery; if you get it right, you win. All the losers get back in an invisible line and wait for their time to be love to arrive.

Well, I'm not going to experience neither love nor rejection if I keep sitting on the sidelines of life.

Primping more than usual, I filled my lips in with plum colored lipstick and teased my wavy hair. Dabbing a little deep-beige powder on my light mocha toned skin; I was ready to face the world.

Observing myself in my oak framed oval shaped full-length mirror, I noticed that my figure seemed toned and in good shape, but I had a big booty for my size. While I was looking at my image, I suddenly knew that I could choose how others see me. I began to think that since I was beautiful, I should be confident; so I held my shoulders back and my head up. Tiffany's sexy swagger crossed my mind and I began to practice a sexy strut. With my chest out, I swayed my hips and swung my arms with a sassy attitude. For approximately three minutes, I practiced walking back and forth across my bedroom floor. I walked like a lady who believed in herself. I think men are attracted to women who have a sexy strut. I've seen the way men have fallen all over Tiffany whenever she does it, I recalled. **Step 4: Do the sexy strut.**

It was open enrollment month for one of Health Gist National's employer groups, West Hill's Savings & Loans. That's when employees of West Hill's Savings & Loans decide on which health insurance plan they'd like to choose for the year.

Mona, one of our new employees received an open enrollment call by mistake, and she was the picture of anxiety when she came to my office for help.

"An open enrollment call came in my queue and I haven't been trained on taking those type of calls yet. The call whisper said, open enrollment," Mona rung her hands. "The potential member keeps asking questions I don't know how to answer. He asked to speak to my supervisor. Could you come please?"

"The call must have been misrouted. I'll take the call, no worries," I munched on a chip and rushed out of my office to her cubicle.

"His name is Maleek," she told me.

Placing her headset on my ears, I sat down at her desk. "Hello Maleek, how are you today?" I opened with a smile in my voice.

"I could be better. First off, Mona doesn't know her head from her feet. What is she doing on the phone anyway? She doesn't know a thing about her job," he vented.

"I apologize for that inconvenience Sir. I'm Mona's supervisor, Joi Glamier, and I'm able to answer your open enrollment questions."

"Why wasn't Mona able to answer my questions? Answer me that," he grumbled.

"She's a new employee who received a misrouted call. Mona hasn't been trained to handle open enrollment calls as of yet, but I would be more than happy to assist you with answering your questions," I explained in an upbeat tone of voice.

I know I sounded like a brownnoser, but it's part of my job. There's a reason why I have a punching bag in my home, to take out my pent-up aggravation on. It's my outlet.

"I'd like my plan options to be explained in detail," he said.

"Do you have your employer group ID number?" I asked.

"As a matter of fact I do, it's 04319D."

"One moment while I pull up your employer's enrollment information." I typed the number into the computer. "Alright, I see your employer is offering two type of plans, a HMO or PPO plan. Which plan are you interested in?"

"I'm not sure. Would you explain the difference between a HMO and a PPO plan?"

"HMO stands for Health Maintenance Organization. On HMO plans, a member must select a Primary Care Physician and a Participating Physician Group. All services must be requested through your selected PCP and approved by the PPG. Being that you have to use doctors within your PPG network of doctors, HMOs can be very restrictive and time consuming," I explained.

"Tell me about the PPO plan and how that works."

"PPO is the acronym for Preferred Provider Organization. On PPO plans you can self refer for most services to any contracted PPO provider. The plan has a $250.00 plan year deductible."

"How does the deductible work?"

"Your deductible is the amount you have to pay off the top before your insurance coverage kicks in. Then, your co-pay and coinsurance amounts will add up towards the calculation of your out of pocket maximum."

"How much is my out of pocket maximum?"

"It's $3500.00 per plan year. If you happen to meet your out of pocket maximum before the year is up, your co-pays and coinsurance amounts will be waived for the rest of the plan year," I concluded.

"I think I understand. This insurance stuff is so freakin' complicated. Does the HMO have a deductible?" he asked.

"No."

"I hate waiting if I need to see a doctor. I think I'll choose the PPO plan this time. You've been great," he sighed.

"Thanks. Any other questions?"

"No. I'd also like to thank you."

"You're very welcome."

"Well, thanks to you I'm all set."

"Have a good day Maleek," I told him in a pleasant tone of voice.

"You too."

After work I dropped by Prescott's Music Store.

Browsing for a few minutes, I selected a music poster and an exquisite b-foot flute and headed for the checkout counter.

While I was waiting in line, I grabbed a directory from off the glass counter and scanned through it. A listing for flute lessons was under the music instruction section, Flute & Voice Info. The music teacher was located in Glendale, CA. I scribbled down the address.

"Did you find everything okay?" the cashier asked.

"Yes I did," I replied.

He added up my items on the cash register. "Will that be cash or credit card?" he asked.

"Credit."

The dark-haired, Italian looking, skinny young man completed my transaction. "Have a good one," he smiled.

"You have a good evening as well," I replied as I exited.

Stepping inside the door of Flute & Voice Info, I didn't see anyone at first. I glanced around to get a feel of the place. The open book on the music stand and the chalkboard looked welcoming. "Cool place," I thought aloud.

On that same note, a male voice from behind stated, "Yeah. I like it too."

Whirling around to face him, I said, "I-I-I didn't see you." Embarrassed that I stammered, I bit my lower lip.

"I was in my office. My name is Curtis Cooper. How may I help you?" he asked with an intriguing smile.

"You look like the singer, Curtis Cooper," my eyes widened.

"Yes, tis I, in the flesh," he smirked.

Swallowing hard, I grew even more wide-eyed. "So you're a music teacher now?"

"Yes. My teen singing sensation years are over. I needed to find another bag, you know."

"Oh Man, how time flies by. You were my favorite recording artist back in 2001," I recalled.

"Those were the good old days, when I was eighteen. I felt like I was on a magic carpet ride. Now it's 2010, and I've come back down to earth."

"I'm still a fan of yours," I smiled warmly.

"Well, I'm glad you are," he mirrored my smile. His gaze was soft as a caress.

Nodding, I could feel my eyes dancing at his handsome face, his dreamy blue eyes, his luscious lips and his manly large hands.

"What exactly did you need?" he asked.

"Oh yes, the reason why I came here. I'm interested in taking flute lessons," I answered. "By the way, my name is Joi Glamier," I put my hand out.

"It's a pleasure to meet you," he nodded as he shook my hand.

"Believe me, the pleasure is all mine. Do you have any opening for Saturday?" I asked.

"I have an opening for one o'clock."

"Then it's all set," I smiled brightly.

"FYI, I charge $30.00 per thirty minute session."

"No worries," I told him.

I lay in bed, staring at the ceiling. I barely got a wink of sleep that night. Thoughts of Curtis Cooper flooded my head. Rolling on to my side, I scrunched the pillow under my neck, and then I restlessly turned to my other side. I found it so surreal that Curtis was now within my reach. I had long admired him from a distance. He's grown from a cute teen singing sensation into a fine, robust, broad-chested Adonis. He looked so hot with his slightly wavy blond hair and his sun-kissed tanned skin. I nearly got lost in his honest eyes, so blue. If the eyes are the windows of the soul, then his must be true, I figured.

"Curtis Cooper is now my flute teacher!" I screamed. "OH WOW!" Some time after that outburst of absolute elation, I slowly drifted to sleep.

*   *   *

Through the day my thoughts persistently drifted to Curtis Cooper. I thought about the first time I saw him; he was singing on TV. As I listened to his R&B CD from 2001, I wondered if he was ever going to make another CD. His voice had a mesmerizing soulful sound.

"Mind on your work," I repeatedly told myself. Instead, I found myself daydreaming about Curtis. I never felt so distracted in my life. I was undeniably infatuated with him.

While I was shopping in the music section of Burton's Books, a handsome stranger who was walking up the aisle bumped into me and all my selections dropped to the floor. He knelled down and scrambled to pick up my books.

"Pardon me. Sorry about that," he looked up into my eyes as he picked up the books.

"That's okay," I replied with a friendly smile.

"Here's your books," he handed them back to me. "So, you play the flute?" he asked with a curious gleam in his eyes.

"Yes," I confidently acknowledged, not letting on that I was a newbie.

"I play the drums in my spare time. It's like a hobby of mine."

"Great, a man with rhythm."

"Hey, you look familiar," he studied my face. "I know I've seen you somewhere before," he quirked an eyebrow questioningly.

"I don't know," I shrugged my shoulders. Some pickup line, I thought.

"Now, I remember. While I was shopping at the grocers the other week, I spoke with your Mom. She showed me your picture," he explained.

"My mom told me she showed my picture to some guy. Now tell me, would you say that you and I meeting like this is coincidental or providential?" I sighed with a pleased expression on my face.

"I don't know. It just may be happenstantial," he chuckled. "All I know is I'd never forget a beautiful face like yours. You look jaw dropping gorgeous," his eyes raked boldly over me.

"Thank you. You look awesome yourself," I gave a tooth paste-ad smile.

"Thanks. I asked your mom for your phone number. I've been meaning to call you."

"You're excused. I can see you've been busy by the title of your selection," I eyed the book in his hand.

"Business management is on my brain," he smiled a winning smile. "Maybe we could go out sometime," he suggested.

"Oh," I looked at him with expressive flirtatious eyes. Nodding approvingly I said, "Your name is Randy right?"

"Yes. My name is Randy Kennedy."

"My name is Joi Glamier. I'm pleased to meet you," I extended a hand to shake his.

"Likewise," he replied. "Would you like to go out on a date with me this weekend?"

"Sure," I smiled.

"How about Saturday evening?"

"That would be great," I answered. I took notice of his high-yellow complexion, his sexy physique and his piercing gray eyes.

"All right then. Where will I pick you up?"

"I live in Valley Village, on 3721 Burbank Avenue."

"Where is that exactly?"

"It's between Studio City and North Hollywood," I explained.

"Alright, it's a date."

"Yes Randy," I smiled. "I've got to run. See ya."

"See ya," he gazed into my eyes.

Walking away, I glanced over my shoulder and noticed Randy watching behind me, so I did my sexy strut.

Once a month I treat myself to one whole day that is filled with nothing but positive energy experiences, to reflect, laugh and restore my soul. On that day, I eat like a vegetarian. I call it, me-time.

Since I had available hours of paid-time-off, I previously arranged to have Friday, June 11th, for my special day of the month.

In preparation for my upcoming date with Randy, I gave myself a facial and painted my nails metallic gold.

I listened to relaxing music all through the day and found myself humming along with contentment.

The next morning, I awoke feeling refreshed. Drawing back the covers, I briskly hopped out of bed. After I brushed my teeth and took a shower, I put on a cute red tank top and a pair of figure-fitting designer blue jeans. On the spur of the moment I decided to go to the beauty salon to get my hair done.

Still debating whether I should put a relaxer in my hair or not, I asked the hairstylist to use a natural method to straighten my hair. While I was having my hair done, I relaxed in the beautician chair, letting my thoughts drift to Curtis Cooper. Anticipating my first flute lesson with him, I wanted to look just right. Then I thought about Randy, who was equally as handsome.

When Kiki was finished with my hair, I was so pleased with the work she had done; I gave her a considerable tip. She had hair styling down to an art form.

It's no mystery that men like women who have incredible hair. **Step 5: Work the hair.**

Chapter 3

Bringing the flute up to my chin, I attempted to play a note.

"It's important to be patient while learning to articulate the desired sound out of a flute. It may take some time, but you must keep practicing and listening for progress," Curtis instructed. "Try to play the C note once again."

With the flute still up to my chin, I played the note.

"Joi, very good. You played a perfect C," he smiled.

It seemed like the room brightened and the temperature rose when he smiled at me. My heart began to race. Nodding, I exhaled.

"We can change the sound of the flute by the way we blow into it, not just by the way we finger the keys. Do you have any questions?"

"Is there a certain music book that you require your flute students to use?"

"I have an extra book in my office that's great for beginners." Curtis walked into his office and came out seconds later with the book. "You can keep it as long as you need it," he stated with a friendly tone of voice.

"Thanks."

A dark beauty sashayed in, wearing a skintight leopard-print dress. Her facial features resembled an Ethiopian's, but she didn't have an accent.

"I have a new flute student." Curtis stood in back of my chair, and placed his hands on my shoulders. "Crystal meet Joi," he politely introduced.

"Hi, I'm Curtis's fiancé," Crystal peered at me as if she were sizing me up.

"Hello," I pasted a smile on my face.

"Crystal, I'll be in the office shortly," he gave her a peck on the lips.

"Sure hon," she replied and pranced into his office.

"Joi, I want you to study the scale on page five of the book I gave you, okay."

"Sure," I replied with a forced smile.

"That's a wrap. Remember to practice," he rushed into his office to be with Crystal.

Carefully disassembling my flute, I placed it back inside its ebony case. I collected my belongings and headed for the door. As I was on my way out, I noticed a posting on Curtis's bulletin board about a poetry workshop. Poetry is romantic. Learning how to write poetry might help my love life, I figured. While I was scribbling down the information, I thought it would be a good idea to expand my extra curricular activities to get my mind off Curtis's engagement.

Step 6: Take up poetry as a personal interest.

At least I have a date with Randy tonight. All is not lost, I thought.

*   *   *

Although I've never been in a serious romantic relationship, that's not to say that I've never had a touch of love in my life.

Some years ago, there was this charming guy I used to go out with named Charles. Well, at the time I didn't want anything more than a platonic friendship, but he had other plans. Charles wanted us to be more than friends. I'd call our get-togethers everything but a date. If I had admitted that we were dating than that would have changed everything. I was in denial, because the magnetism between us was ecstatic.

The first time I saw Charles I said, "Whoa," to myself. He looked so fine. His sexy scent thrilled my senses. One time he spontaneously placed his arm around my body and a warm, sweet, electrical sensation that I had never felt before surged through my anatomy. His touch made me feel so good and alive. After that, I longed for him to touch me again.

Eventually, the cares of life led us in different paths.

As I recall, I thought that love should happen whenever I became ready for it, but love doesn't always happen within our neatly planned schedules. Sometimes love comes unexpectedly.

At times I reminisce about Charles and shed a tear or two. I miss the way his eyes sparkled with interest when he'd look at me. I regret that I never encouraged his advances, because now he's married to someone else. Every time I hear Joycia's song, "Be Mine" I think of him. I sort of loved him, I guess. I never gave our relationship a chance to grow. I know it could've been beautiful.

*   *   *

After I put on my elegant sleeveless red dress and matching high-heels, I posed in front of the mirror like a model, to get the full effect. Then I carefully filled in my lips with deep cocoa lipstick.

Randy picked me up in a black Mercedes Benz. He looked extremely fine, decked out in his slate blue designer shirt and brown dress slacks. The cologne he wore had a charming scent.

"Guess where we're going," Randy said to me as he drove onto the freeway entrance.

"Give me a hint."

He song a verse of Joycia's hit song, "The One You Love."

"We're going to a music store?" I giggled.

"No honey, it ain't even funny. I'm taking you to a Joycia Concert."

"Wow, I'm surprised," I looked at him with flirtatious eyes.

"What were you expecting, Willy Burger or something?" he looked at me out of his peripheral vision.

"I don't know."

"I always show the women I go out with a good time," he frankly stated.

I smiled at him.

"I don't do dinky dates. I'm class personified," he bragged.

For a Saturday evening, the traffic wasn't unbearable. Although, I still appreciated the added convenience of the carpool lane.

We arrived at the Upamp Auditorium parking lot, which looked filled to capacity. Fortunately, we found a space on the lot that wasn't too far away. I enjoyed the walk.

"Joycia is new on the scene, but judging by the size of the crowd here to see her, she's rising to the top like cream," Randy said as we were walking to the auditorium.

"I like her music," I nodded.

Moments later we found our tenth-row seats.

There she was, on stage with the spotlight on her. Joycia was sitting on a round stool with her acoustic guitar in her hand. She was dressed in a rust multi-colored sexy outfit. She looked up at the audience and the cheers of faithful fans cut through the silence before she uttered a word.

She played an upbeat arpeggio finger-style accompaniment as she sang "The One You Love." Joycia really knew how to draw the audience in to her. I couldn't help but clap along as she performed. She kept perfect tempo with her tapping foot. The songstress sounded more beautiful than a songbird. I listened attentively as she sang a new song I never heard before called, "Keep On Loving Me," it was brilliant. During her performance of "Be Mine," Randy placed his arm around my shoulders. I enjoyed the whole concert. I'm still wondering how she got a base groove out of an acoustic guitar. I loved her live performance.

"I'm hungry. Let's get something to eat," Randy told me as we exited the Upamp Auditorium.

"So, which place are you thinking of?"

"We can go to Twilight. It's a fine restaurant on Ventura Boulevard. The food there is very tasteful. And besides I want to show off my beautiful date. Look at you, lady in red, turning heads. I want the world to see me with you," he raved about me. Randy looked at me as if he adored me.

Pretending to be bold, I twirled around and struck a pose like a movie star. Someone told me I looked like one before. Actors pretend all the time. I was willing to forgo my shyness to have a honest-to-goodness man in my life. Looking into his adorable gray eyes I said, "Let's go."

He placed his arm around me, and we walked back to his car in the cool of the evening. His touch had a warm possessive feel to it.

Stepping to the entrance of Twilight restaurant, Randy maneuvered to open the door for me. "Ladies first," he gestured with his arm.

"Thank you," I said. Then I strutted inside the upscale restaurant with a little twist in my hips. I had my smooth and sexy on tight.

A busy waiter set us up at a table. "I'll be right back to take your orders," he hurried away.

Looking down at my menu I considered the options.

Randy looked at his menu for a nanosecond and placed it down on the table. "I know what I want."

"Ready to order?" the waiter asked.

"Yes we are," Randy looked up and answered.

The waiter took Randy's order.

"I'll have the same," I told the waiter.

"You must think I have good taste," he smirked.

"You're out with me aren't you?"

He chuckled.

"I've been here once before, but I've never had the food we've ordered tonight. I hope it's good."

"I've eaten here many times. Trust me, the food is good," he reassured me with a wink of an eye.

"Thanks again for taking me to the Joycia concert. It was a real treat."

He nodded with a pleasant expression on his face.

"How did you know she was performing in the area?"

"I'm an avid fan of Joycia's. I stay up to date about her latest events by checking her Website, Joycianow.com."

"I think I'll browse her Website too. I liked what she had on," I smiled.

"You look a little like her," he smiled at me.

"I do?"

The waiter removed the plates off the serving tray and placed the delectable food before us.

I sampled the sweet and sour rice salad.

"How do you like it?' he asked.

"It's interestingly good," I replied.

Randy ate his food faster than you could say the word, "supercalifragilisticexpialidocious."

"Joi, tell me about yourself," his eyes were sharp and assessing.

"I'm a lover of the arts. I play the flute. I'm a Customer Service Supervisor at Health Gist National. I attend church from time to time."

"Sounds nice," he nodded.

"So what is Randy Kennedy all about?" I asked.

"I'm the owner of Kennedy Construction. I'm a Catholic. I'm good at playing the drums."

"I'd like to hear you play sometime."

"That can be arranged. I play drums for a group called Rapalicious. We've done a few gigs."

"Great."

"I'll invite you to our next gig," he smiled.

"I'd come," I nodded. "What is the longest romantic relationship you've ever been in?"

"Hold up, let me ask the questions."

"Why was that question a sore subject for you? Give me real talk, not bullshit."

"Around a month ago, I caught my girlfriend of three years cheating on me," his light skin turned a reddish tone. He became irritated.

"Aw, I'm sorry that happened," I empathized.

"She was a fuckin' whore." A tear rolled down his cheek.

"Are you alright?" I reached out and touched the back of his hand. "Here," I handed him a napkin from the table.

"I'll get myself together in a minute," he exhaled.

We didn't ask each other any more questions for the rest of the evening. I focused on my food and ate every bit of it. It was delicious.

Overall, the date I had with Randy was enchanting. I think I'm in like with him already. He behaved like a gentleman in every since of the word.

The next morning I was awakened by the sound of my doorbell. I hopped out of bed and ran down the hallway into the living room and looked out the peephole to see who was at the door. "Just a minute," I hollered out.

Running into the bathroom, I brushed my teeth in a quick minute. I splashed water on my face and grabbed my emergency wig. I always kept it on standby for urgent situations. I raced back to my front door.

Opening the door, I greeted, "Good morning Randy." My eyes darted to the clock on the wall. "It's 6:25 in the morning," I stated with an annoyed tone of voice as I stepped out on the porch.

"Well excuse me for paying you a visit," he snapped.

"Randy, I like to sleep late on the weekends," I sighed.

He exposed his genitalia.

Placing a hand over my eyes, I asked, "Why did you do that?"

"My other dates usually invite me in for a nightcap," he said in a serious tone of voice.

"Would you put it back in your pants please?"

"Alright," he grumbled.

"I don't do booty calls or casual romps," I told him.

"Say what!" he squealed and looked around over his shoulder.

"Randy, don't trip. You just need to slow your roll a bit."

"What?" He brushed the palm of his hand backwards over his hair.

"I'm going to wait until I'm ready. Okay."

"I can respect that you want to wait. Although, another part of me wants to play a game of one on one with you."

"We've only dated once. I figure what's the hurry?" I eyed him.

"I actually dated a sexy-nerd who's gonna make me wait," he pouted. "Do you have any plans today?"

"I plan on going to church."

"That's right, a church girl," he nodded. "In the meantime, I'll go home and take a cold shower. See ya." He ran to his white pickup truck and drove away.

I appreciated the lovely date that I had with Randy, but there was something left to be said about decency. I wasn't for sale.

* * *

During my lunchtime, I usually take a walk from Health Gist National to Maury's Cafe. It's practically next-door. Tiffany is a manager there. Sometimes she takes her lunch when I come in; and we sit at a window table and chat about anything that comes to mind.

Stepping up to the counter, I sat down on a barstool. "It smells so good in here," I smiled. "So how are you today, Miss Tiffany?"

"Oh I'm having a shitty day," she frowned. "I had to fire one of my girls, because I overheard her being rude to one of the customers. I wouldn't have believed she had such a foul attitude if I hadn't seen it with my own two eyes. There are too many cafes closing down to tolerate an employee who gives bad customer service. The customer told me that he was never gonna come back here again. I had to apologize over and over."

"Tell me about it girlfriend. You can catch more bees with honey than castor-oil," I smirked.

She laughed. "Girl shut up. I'm serious," she said.

"I'm serious too."

"So what will you have today?"

"La la la. Let's see. I'll have my usual." I replied.

"Coffee twirl blast, coming right up."

"There you go," I placed my credit card on the counter.

Tiffany placed my shake down on the counter. "I'm taking my lunch now!" she yelled through the double doors back to the kitchen area.

"All right," a male voice replied.

"Come on let's go to a table. Firing an employee always makes me feel bottomed out. Tasha was like one of my peeps," she chattered on as she led the way past the tables of talking customers, until we sat down at an empty table in the back.

"You're just having one of those days. Guess what?" I asked as I sat down at the table.

"What?"

"I had a date last Saturday with a very attractive man," I told her.

"Where did you meet him?"

"My Mom sort of hooked me up with him."

"Joi, has it come to this?" she shook her head.

"Sometimes Mothers know, then again, sometimes they don't. The date went fine, but the next morning he came over my house for some nookie."

Tiffany laughed. "Did you give him some?" she asked with extreme interest.

"No, because I didn't want him to get the wrong impression about me. I read in a magazine article that a man knows by the eighth date which file he puts a woman in: the platonic friendship file, the slut file, or the marriage file. I'm aiming to be thought of as marriage material, okay."

"Girl, I don't have your willpower," she shook her head. "How about just having some fun?"

"What if he turns out to be someone I want. I don't want to blow it by being too easy. Part of a man's instinct is to be a hunter. Men tend to disregard things that are easy to get. Do you know where I'm going with this?"

"You might be right. But women out number men, and I'll do anything to keep a man. It's so many woman out there who wouldn't say no if a man wanted to get up in their grill."

"If all he's looking for is a loose booty, then I wouldn't want him anyway. I want a meaningful relationship, not just sex."

Tiffany's way of going about snagging a man was a cut—to-the-chase thing, but would that kind of carrying on help her keep him in the end? She's dated a whole slew of men, and none of her relationships have lasted over a year.

Step 7: Don't be too easy.

"Are you gonna see him again?" she asked.

"Maybe, maybe not. Something tells me I haven't seen the last of him. He asked me about my plans for the day, the last time I spoke with him."

"Do you have any plans for the weekend?"

"I've started taking flute lessons with Curtis Cooper. He's the one who sung, "I Love Lovin' You." That song was my favorite."

"I remember him. They used to call him Blue-Eyed Soul. He had a silver tongue with his fine self."

"Yes, but he's my music teacher now," I bragged.

"What's up with you? I usually have to beg you to get out and do things."

"Tiffany, I've decided to let love and life in," I said in an as a matter of fact tone. "So do you have any plans?"

"Max and I are an item now," she smiled. "So I'll be going out with him this weekend."

"I'll wait and see if Randy asks me out again," I smiled to myself.

I reckon most people would think it's odd that Tiffany and I are best friends, because we don't always see eye to eye. But she helps me stay in touch with what's going on in the twenty-first century. Maybe we're friends because we are different. She encourages me to live life. And I'm like her voice of reason that she desperately needs at times.

*   *   *

I watched a classic film that actually left me teary-eyed. You know, the kind of romantic movie that makes you wonder what happened next, even though you realize it's fictional. I love to watch movies that make my imagination run.

A lot of movies nowadays have people who are barely acquainted having sex. Scenes of groping couples doing-it have become boringly redundant. Where's the romance? Can the parties at least be acquainted? I'm a traditional heterosexual who prefers to watch love scenes limited to two participants, one of each gender.

Why do some people expect a new relationship to be consummated immediately? Maybe it's just the signs of the times. There used to be a day when couples took the time to get to know each other, fall in love, and get married etcetera. It seems to me that couples stayed together a lot longer back when love was pursued in a courtly manner.

I only hope that I'll remain strong enough to not compromise my standards. The ways of the world is like a whirlpool; I'm trying not to get sucked in. I don't want to become a stranger to myself. I was so tempted when Randy showed his penis to me. He looked so hot. The steaming feeling I felt for him relentlessly lingered on.

Chapter 4

I was about to sit down on my black leather recliner to eat a bowl of fruit salad when I heard the phone ring. I hurried to the phone and picked up the receiver.

"Yes," I answered.

"Hi Joi. This is Gege."

"Oh hi Gege," I greeted in a singsong voice.

"I hope I didn't catch you at a bad time."

"No it's fine. What's up?"

"I want you to promise me that you won't breath a word of what I'm about to tell you to anyone," she began.

"I won't say a word to anyone about it. Word is bond," I told her.

"I need someone to talk to, really."

"Are you okay?" I asked.

"I'd like to say that I am, but I'm not," she tried to stifle a sob. "I need to get this off my chest and let out my feelings. Brent really hurt me. I've tried to talk to him about what he's done, but it's like talking to a brick wall. He's still in denial about it."

"Let's rewind and start from the beginning."

"In my heart I want to let it go. I think it might help me to move on if I talk about it."

"Take your time."

"I'm gonna say it. Here goes," she hesitated. "Brent has been fronting like he's straight, when he is really gay. He's been living a double life called the down-low."

"I don't understand how a man like Brent could be like that, because he seems so manly-like," I told her.

"That's just it, men who are on the down-low want to seem manly or heterosexual in order to fool unsuspecting women. DL men do not want to be classified as gay. They want the best of both worlds. They want to appear to be heterosexual in public and secretly creep around with other men on the side," Gege informed.

"I've heard of the term DL before, but I didn't know it was like that. How did you find out?"

"Brent's best friend named Victor turned out to be his secret bed-buddy," she blurted out.

"Say what!"

"I came home unexpectedly and caught the two of them in bed together. Girl, my heart stopped. I was devastated."

"This is scary. Were there any telltale signs that you can think of?"

"Brent and Victor would spend a lot of time at the gym together. He'd comment on how good-looking certain men are sometimes. Let's see what else, oh, he was very secretive. Whenever we'd have sex he'd do it in my ass most of the time. We've only had cock in coochie sex a few times, and it was passionless. I should have realized that something was off-centered about our relationship. I guess I just wanted a man in my life," she sighed.

"Ah crap."

"I've been lied to, cheated on and exposed to disease. I'm going through something right now," she cried. "I feel like I've been used like a garbage can by that asshole. I was about to marry a stranger who had no regard for my safety or well-being."

"Gege, I'm sorry this happened to you. It's good you didn't marry him."

"To be honest with you, I never felt peace about marring him anyway. That was God trying to tell me something."

"I always trust my gut feeling."

"See, I thought I was going to have a successful doctor for a husband. But it turned out that Brent is full of bullshit."

"We need to protect ourselves and value ourselves enough to get to know the man we may have sex with. Having sex can be dangerous these days, with all the dirty diseases out there. It could mean a matter of life or death," I interjected.

"That's right, cause many African American women have contracted HIV from brothas on the down-low and that's low-down."

"Why down-low men have to be so sneaky and evil about it? They're hurting innocent women, and evidently they don't give a damn. I had been thinking straight is straight and gay is gay."

"It's not necessarily a bisexual thing. DL is something different."

"Well you've schooled me," I told her.

Step 8: Beware of men on the down-low.

"Oou girl, I feel like a burden has lifted."

"That was too much to hold inside. Thanks for letting me know about it. I needed to know."

"We've helped each other. I needed someone to talk to. That shit needed to be brought to the light. Thanks for being there."

After Gege and I hung up, I resolved that I would be open-minded about dating other races. That will make my odds of finding the right man that much greater. Everyone is of the human race anyhow.

Nikki came to my office and said, "Sup call."

A long sigh was my first response, because I had already taken three escalated supervisor calls that day. "Did you do everything you could to turn the call around?" I asked as I made my way to Nikki's cubicle to take the call.

"Yes. But she insisted on speaking to a supervisor," she whined.

I put her headset on my ears and sat down. "Hello, you requested to speak with a supervisor," I opened.

"My name is Mrs. Calwell. I met my $500.00 PPO deductible! I should not have $2.95 left on my deductible!" the member vented at full volume in my ear.

"Excuse me, my name is Joi Glamier, Nikki's supervisor. I can handle your issue. Let's see what we can do," I told her with a smile in my voice as I eyed the computer screen, researching the member's claims.

"Nikki sure couldn't handle my issue. She fussed at me like she was talking to someone out on the street or something," she complained.

"Ms. I apologize for that. I will coach her."

"She needs it," she giggled softly.

"My next step is to review your claims and get down to the bottom of your concern," I reassured with an upbeat tone of voice.

"Thank you," the member sighed.

"No problem," I replied. But I felt like telling her, "Lady get a life and get off the damn line. If you don't have a life, I do." Geez laweez!

"You can see that I paid my deductible right?"

"I can see all the claims that we have processed for you and all the deductible amounts that have been applied to each date of service." One by one, I discussed each claim with her and calculated the applied deductible amounts.

"See, I told you I paid it," she said.

"Yes, you have met your $500.00 deductible. The $2.95 amount is actually your 10% coinsurance that you owe to your doctor," I explained.

"So that's what that amount is," she mused. "Oh, I see that on my EOB."

"Is there anything else?" I asked.

"No. That's all for now."

"Have a good day Mrs. Calwell."

"You do the same."

Standing up from Nikki's desk, I advised, "You need to practice remaining calm. Even when the member is irate, it's never okay to raise your voice at a member."

"All right, but she cussed at me," she pouted.

"Nikki, you know the protocol to follow if a member uses coarse language."

"I'll do better."

"Alright now. You've just given me your word," I made a mental note.

*   *   *

It was such a lovely day, that late afternoon. The sun was sparkling through the trees. I made it back to my home in Valley Village. While I was opening my gate to drive into my yard, I thought about how I used to dream of owning a home with a fenced in yard.

"Hey Joi," my next-door neighbor greeted.

"Hi Mrs. Crabtree," I waved.

When I got promoted to Customer Service Supervisor, my salary was raised 40%. I managed my money wisely and saved up enough to make my own dream come true. I bought this nice place with the added trimmings of a fenced in yard.

I'm even able to plant fruits and vegetables in my garden out back, without stray dogs taking leaks on them. Imagine that. In the city, a fenced in yard is considered a luxury.

Walking into my living room, I placed my purse on the extravagant transparent glass table. Slipping off my high-heel pumps with a sigh of relief, I began to unwind from my day.

Heading into the kitchen, I opened the fridge and poured myself an ice-cold glass of orange juice. On a warm day it hits the spot.

Moments later, I thought of the music book that Curtis gave me. Leaning down, I took the book out of my music bag and reclined as I studied.

"Hey Tiff, I just called to let you know that I'm not going to walk over for lunch today. I'm gonna grab a bite to eat from the break-room here."

"I wish you were coming. I mean, I need to sort my thoughts about Max," she sighed.

"What about him? I think he's so not worth your time," I told her.

"Don't be bias before you here me out. I love Max, but he's the kinkiest man I've ever been with. It's something he wants me to do with him that I don't think I'm ready for."

"What is it?"

"Well, Max asked me to have a threesome with him."

"How come that doesn't surprise me? He's too friendly if you ask me. Did he say who else he wanted in this threesome?" I asked with sarcasm.

"It's some woman he knows," she choked up. "Joi, I don't want to lose him," she said in a desperate tone of voice.

"Tiffany, that type of behavior is too risky. You could get infected with a STD. You look good. You can do better than him," I reasoned with her.

"When my 30th birthday rolled around, I began to think I needed to take what I can get."

"In your heart do you think he's the one you should settle for?"

"Maybe, maybe not. All I know is I've had the best sex with him. He drives me crazy."

"Everything that feels good ain't good for you. And what about love."

"I love him and I want him to love me. So I'm gonna do what I have to do to keep him," she said with a determined tone of voice.

"If I were you, I'd have Max show me his HIV negative certificate. I want you to be okay," I told her.

"I know. I'll think about what you told me."

* * *

"Special delivery for you." One of the staff sat a bouquet of lavender-violet roses on my desk, and I was electrified. "Sweet," she said.

"Oh wow," I was in awe of the beautiful roses. It was an unexpected, thoughtful, romantic gift.

Carlton, a supervisor from another department on the 5th floor, poked his head into my office. "Kudos. I see you have an admirer," he said as he stood in the doorway.

"And so I do." I picked out a rose and smelled it as I read the little card, "Thinking of you. Let's go out again. Signed Randy."

"FYI, lavender-violet roses means love at first sight," he told me.

"That's great," I beamed.

"Who is he?" he asked.

"A guy I've dated."

"I didn't know you were single."

"Now you know," I replied.

"Any man would be lucky to have you," he told me.

"Thanks," I gave a smile.

"See you at the two o'clock meeting in the big conference room."

"Oops, I almost forgot,"

"Come back down to earth and join us," he laughed.

"Alright, I'm back from cloud eight," I looked up at him. "See you," I smirked.

Looking at the Westking College map, I finally found classroom number 217. I was eager to start the poetry workshop. Walking inside the class, I noticed a variety of personalities. I found a seat near the front section of the room. Other students trickled in after me. Then I saw Curtis Cooper rush into the class. He raised his eyebrows when he saw me. He sat down at the desk next to mine, to the right.

"Hello there," I greeted.

"Hi you," Curtis smiled.

"So where's your girl, Crystal?" I asked.

"Oh, she's not into poetry writing. As for me, I write poetry because it helps me sort through my feelings. I'm a songwriter too. I still produce songs for the industry," he stated.

I nodded attentively.

After everyone signed the attendance sheet, Ms. Sinclair, the poetry teacher, stood up in front of the class with a melancholy expression on her face. "Is there anyone here who has an original poem that you would like to share with the class?"

Curtis raised his index finger. "I'd like to share a poem," he volunteered.

> I reached out
> to catch a piece of love
> in the palm of my hand.
> Unable to elude me
> I chased it down and
> we went for a walk
> in the sand.

"That was quite good," Ms. Sinclair clapped.

The class nodded in agreement as we applauded.

"You're phenomenal," I smiled at him.

He blushed.

Reaching into my purse I pulled out my new burgundy journal and placed it on my desk.

Another student raised her hand, "My name is Lakita," she cleared her throat. "Here's my poem . . ."

> Moves, grooves
> fashions
> shoes,
> ever changing
> rearranging
> in and out
> life's moods.

The class applauded.

"That was cute," the instructor clapped.

A slow smile spread across Lakita's face.

"Whatever is in your soul, will spill out on paper as you write from that place. A poet sees the heart of things, thereto expressing what's behind the feelings of love, excitement, happiness, sadness, etcetera," Ms. Sinclair explained.

I picked up my pencil, ready to write.

"You will need to take notes for the following exercise. Please have pencil and paper ready."

My eyes glanced over at Curtis as he opened his brown leather journal and scribbled with his pen.

"This exercise is called mindrushing. It will help increase your poetic creativity. At the top of a blank page, write the word special. Then, you will write whatever comes to mind about that word. Exploring your feelings, you're to write words for three minutes. Afterwards you are to underline every word or phrase that you think would work in a poem. Finally, you'll write a poem using the words you've underlined."

The class scribbled notes.

"I'm setting the timer for three minutes. Ready set mindrush," she said.

Every word or phrase that came to mind about the word special, I nervously scribbled as fast as I could. I was trying to beat the clock. I even thought about the date I had with Randy and the flowers.

The timer sounded off like a ringing bell. "Time's up. Now underline every word you'd like to use in poetic verse. I'll give you a few minutes to work on your poems," she smiled and sat back down at her desk.

Moments later, Ms. Sinclair asked, "Is there anyone who has finished a poem from the exercise?"

I raised my hand immediately.

She gave me a nod.

"The name of my poem is called "Special Moments,"" I read.

> Beautiful conversation
> laughter
> special moments
> out with you.
> Thoughtful surprises
> my love rises
> to kiss you.

"Whoa!" Ms. Sinclair shouted. "Great love poem," she clapped.

The class enthusiastically applauded.

I gave myself a pat on the back.

"Whom did you write that poem about?" Curtis boldly asked in front of the class.

Shyness crept back in, "A lo, love interest," I stuttered.

He nodded with a peculiar expression on his face.

I wondered about Curtis's interest in my poetry.

"There's an important thing I want you to keep in mind class, a poem doesn't necessarily have to rhyme, although it can," she happily taught.

She went on, "Another thing, if the word special didn't inspire you enough; try using another word with the exercise. I want to awaken the poet in each and every one of you."

Tiffany reached for my burgundy journal on top of my bedroom dresser. "I didn't know you kept a journal," she flipped through the pages.

"My inner most thoughts are in there," I crossed the room, snatched the journal away and held it to my chest.

"Oou, what are you writing about?" Tiffany eyed me.

"Girl, you're trying to dip all up in my cool-aid, trying to know all the flavors."

"Tell me what's up. Look at you. You're practically glowing. I know someone has got you moist," she fished.

"Maybe, maybe not," I smirked and sat on the edge of my bed.

"It's me, your best friend. An enquiring mind would like to know," she sat down on a stool.

"The guy I went out with sent a beautiful bouquet of lavender-violet roses to my office. I felt like I was being wooed. I sort of like him, but I'll see how it turns out."

"So when do you think is the right time to stop withholding the booty?"

"In my heart I'll know."

"Maybe I've been giving up my ass too soon. I've yet to receive a bouquet of roses at work. Keep me posted on Romeo," her eyebrows rose. "How did you like your flute lesson with Curtis?"

"It was okay. Guess what?"

"What?"

"He's engaged," I sighed.

"So. She does not own him until they make the vows to each other," Tiffany stated.

"Your posture is tall," Curtis rubbed my back. "I hear more sound control," he instructed in a businesslike manner.

"I've been studying the flute book you gave me," I smiled.

"You're showing promise," he smiled as he said those encouraging words.

His smile was so charming. I slightly lost my breath. "I'm glad you think so," my eyes widened. "Could you play a song for me on your flute?" I asked.

"Is there any song in particular that you'd like to hear?" Curtis asked as he walked into his office to retrieve his flute.

"Um, I don't know. Play whatever you like," I waited with anticipation.

"One of my favorites, is a jazz piece by Hubert Laws, called, "Restoration." Are you familiar with him?" He asked as he assembled his flute.

"I've heard of him," I replied.

Curtis played the song with a soul soothing dynamic sound. Listening to his brilliant techniques made my love for the flute grow even more. That's not to say, that I didn't adore the flute before. You just would've had to been there. As he played I felt like I was carried away. Humming along, I imagined that I too would become as skilled in my own flute renditions. I could see it in my mind's eye.

I'll see if my next date with Randy will go as smooth.

Chapter 5

"What's up? I thought you were feelin' me," Randy questioned with a puzzled expression on his face.

"Good things come to those who wait. So, I'm waiting until the right man comes along," I replied.

"The right man just might be lookin' at ya," he gazed at me.

"Who knows?" I shrugged my shoulders.

"Here's your order," the waiter placed the food on the table.

"Thanks. I'm ready to eat," he said.

"It sure smells good," I commented as I took a bite. "Mm, it is good," I nodded.

"That, it is," he agreed as he chewed.

"This is a nice restaurant. It's only a block away from where I live, but I've never been here."

"I found out about this place on the Internet. It had an A rating. This is my first time here too," he glanced around at the interior of the restaurant.

While I was looking around the place, I noticed a beautiful painting of an orchestra hanging on the wall. There were two flute players in the masterpiece. "That's a lovely painting," I commented.

He eyed the painting and nodded.

Smiling at Randy, I chewed a bite of food.

"Joi, I want to make love to you. I'm feeling so sick about this," he sighed and peered at me intently.

The smoldering flame I saw in his eyes startled me. My heart jolted and my pulse pounded. He was so compelling. His magnetism was so potent. My mind told me to resist, but my body felt charmed. I squirmed inside, feeling the heat. "You don't know me like that yet," I blurted out. "Let's get to know each other better," I suggested.

Step 9: Get to know each other.

"I've already told you about myself," he let out a frustrated breath. "What do you mean?" he asked.

"I'd like to know your likes, your dislikes, your beliefs, your wishes . . ."

"You already know I'm Catholic, and you know what I'm wishing for," he said with a frustrated tone of voice.

"Can't we talk for a while, before we get into having sex?" I looked at him, my eyes curious and filled with longing.

"I know you want me."

"Guess my age," I made a feeble attempt to change the subject.

"You look around my age. I'm twenty-nine. I guess you're around twenty-eight," he assessed.

"I'm thirty-eight," I divulged.

"Unbelievable, you look so young," he mused.

"Does our difference in age bother you?" I questioned, rigidly waiting for an answer.

"I don't mind, I still feel the same about you baby." He gazed at me with bedroom-eyes of gray and took my hand and kissed it on the back.

I inhaled sharply at the contact. I felt like a breathless girl of eighteen.

He rested his large masculine hand atop mines.

"Our difference in age doesn't bother me either."

"We're both adults," he sipped his drink.

"If you'll be patient with me, we can see where this will go."

He nodded. "Is it true about what they say about the quiet ones?" he narrowed his eyes at me.

"What?" my eyebrows raised.

"You're probably one of those nasty closet-freaks, with your sexy self," Randy accused.

So much for conversation. "That done it. Randy, I thought I liked you. Now, I'm not so sure. What you just said to me was very inappropriate. I'm a lady, and I'd appreciate it if you would treat me with some consideration for my views. Thanks for the dinner." I wiped my mouth with a napkin and threw it down on the table. "I'll call a cab." Grabbing my purse, I dismissed myself from the table.

"Joi, don't leave," he reached out for me. "Stuck up snooty ass," he mumbled.

Walking away, I took out my cell phone to call a taxicab.

I behaved as though I was upset about Randy's desire for me. I figured there would be a time and place to express those feelings. I know we can't always turn off our emotions like turning off a faucet. The truth is, I was flattered by his interest in me, but if Randy would slow his roll I'd be able to tell if he's good for me or not, I thought.

That night I sat down on my couch, opened my journal and penned a poem by lamplight.

It's Not Time

You look at me
as though you like
what you see.
You want to make love to me.
It's not time to get physical.
Do you wanna know
me though?
I have individuality.
There's more to me
than what you see.
We all have beliefs
and doubts.
Let's see each other
inside out.
If you wanna rock
my world,
you'll look deep inside
for the pearl.
I want to know where
this is gonna go.
So let's take it nice and slow.
I'm saving myself
for one who
loves me for me.

* * *

Sipping on my strawberry breakfast shake, I walked the floor of the call center. "Late again," I cringed. "Darren, after you login, sign out on meeting, and report to my office," I spoke out to one of the associates in my department as he was headed to his cubicle.

When he arrived in my office, he sat forward and looked at me attentively.

"Darren, you're scheduled to began your shift at 8:00 a.m. not 8:15. Why are you repeatedly late?" I calmly asked.

"My bus is always late," his dark eyebrows slanted in a frown.

"Your attendance records show that you've been tardy 24 times since the beginning of this year, and I must take action."

"Joi, I'm trying so hard to be here on time. And you know when it comes to work I give 100%."

"When it comes to getting the job done, you are one of our best associates. We need you to be dependable as well. That's why we're having this conversation," I stated firmly.

"I can't lose my job. I have to support my son," he gasped.

"If you truly need your job, this excessive tardiness has to stop right now. My supervisor has accused me of being insubordinate because I have failed to write you up for this," I exasperated.

"I'm sorry. Please give me another chance," a tear rolled down his cheek.

"I'm coaching you about this, and I also have to write you up for being tardy today. If I have to write you up two more times this year, you will be terminated. Would you like to change your time schedule to come in at 8:30? I'm trying to work with you."

"If you could change my schedule to 8:30 to 5:00, that would work," he nodded.

"Alright. Adrian wants to come in earlier, so I'll trade your schedule with hers. I'll notify her by email of the shift change. But you still need to catch the same bus. Don't be late anymore. I hope I've made this perfectly clear."

"Yes. Oh yes. Thank you so much for giving me another chance," he swiped at a tear.

"Don't let me down," I eyed him.

"I won't."

Tilting the computer screen, I checked the service levels. "OMG! We have 21 calls in queue. Darren, I need you on the phone right now," I told him with a since of urgency.

"Sure thing," he rushed out of my office.

Tiffany showed up at my door in exercise gear, which wasn't usual. "Joi, come to the fitness center with me, so we can get a good workout," she paced the floor.

Penning a poem in my journal, I glanced up and looked back at my book. "I have some things to do. Couldn't we go to the gym some other time?" I asked.

"So this evening is out?" she pouted.

"Yes," I nodded looking up at her.

"Joi, you used to always have time for me. Since you've been dating, I barely see you anymore."

"That's not true. Well, excuse me for trying to have a life," I snapped. She threw a small coach pillow at me.

"Girl, I know you didn't throw a pillow at me."

"Yes I did," she giggled. "Joi, come on," she coaxed. "I need to tighten up my game for Max, and I'd like your support. It's getting harder for me to keep a man, and I don't know why," she sighed.

Glancing at the clock, I said, "All right. Besides, I need to make sure my game stays tight," I smirked.

"Let's go then. What are you writing anyway?"

"Poetry. It's a new fascination of mine."

"Poetry," she parroted. "Are you almost done?" she impatiently asked.

"I'm done." Thrilled with my poem, I rushed to put my journal away and suit up for a workout.

Scanning the room over, before I walked inside, I spotted Curtis already seated to the right of the class. I selected a desk not far from his.

"Hi," I cheerfully waved as I walked to a desk.

"Hi back," Curtis smiled. Crystal didn't want me to come, but I came anyway," he added with a grim tone.

"The nerve of her."

"Tell me about it," he remarked.

"If you want to be a poet, it's important to write down your feelings the moment you feel them. Play with words and write them as you see life," Ms. Sinclair instructed.

Pulling out my journal, I turned to a blank page ready to create.

Ms. Sinclair wrote instructions on the dry-erase board, about how to write Rondelet styled poetry. She gave us a lot of details. "If you're daring try to write a Rondelet," she told us.

Imagining my dream man, I felt a wave of inspiration and began to write.

> When you're near me
> the days seem brighter, I feel new.
> When you're near me
> life seems clearer, I feel so free.
> The dreams I'm dreaming might come true,
> love's fulfillment comes into view,
> when you're near me.

Curtis's cell phone rung and he quickly stepped outside the class to take the call. He left his journal open on his desk.

Being somewhat curious about Curtis, I tossed my pencil near his desk to have a valid reason to walk over and sneak a peak at his poetry. There it was, his inner most thoughts glaring from his open journal. I speed-read it. Hmmm, I thought.

"Joi, looking for something?" Ms. Sinclair asked.

"I dropped my pencil," I picked it up and showed it to her. Then I scurried back to my desk without a second to spare.

Curtis re-entered the classroom.

Oh dear, I mused. I was in shock about the poem Curtis wrote. Let's see if I can remember it correctly, I thought.

> Should I love you?
> I am someone else's love flame.
> Should I love you?
> I know I want to be with you.
> I wonder if you feel the same.
> Are you available to claim?
> Should I love you?

Yes, that's it. He actually wrote a perfect Rondelet.

I can't believe I did that. That was a little naughty to sneak a peak at his journal. I shouldn't have done that. Oh well, I giggled to myself.

I wonder who he's crushing on? Hmmm, I thought.

Chapter 6

Checking the Dream Match Website, I found that I had received emails from various guys. Two of the men were handsome, and I also liked their profiles. So, I sent a response back to them.

Well, Terence and I seemed to click. I had been doing some online chatting with him. He seemed okay. He was a good looking, curly haired black men, who was thirty-two. He worked as a Paralegal in downtown LA.

I arranged for us to meet for a date. Maybe this could be the start of something special, I thought.

My Mom wasn't happy that I had met a man over the Internet. She became so worried when I told her I was planning to go out on a date with Terrence. She told me, "The news says, that there are predators on those types of sites. I know there's someone better for you. Did you ever talk with Randy?"

"Yes, but I'm not sure about Randy. I'll be cautious," I assured her.

"To reach the higher notes blow into the flute faster, aiming your stream out. The higher notes takes more air," Curtis explained.

Nodding with the flute to my chin, I hit the note with a sigh of relief.

"With consistent practice, you'll be able to play any note you want," he encouraged.

I made a mental note of his supportive words. "I'll keep practicing," I nodded.

"Good. I want you to reach your goals in life," he placed his hand on my shoulder. His touch was oddly soft and caressing.

He seemed to have good hygiene. I liked his scent. Looking in his eyes, blue as the summer sky, I found reassurance.

Curtis looked at me with a smile as intimate as a kiss.

"You're an excellent teacher," I complimented him.

"You're a good student." Curtis had an easygoing expression on his face, but it seemed to mask some deeper emotion.

"Crystal is lucky to have you." I wouldn't mind being in her shoes, I thought.

"Sometimes I don't feel so lucky to have her," he confided.

Could the poem he wrote be about me? My pulse quickened at the speculation.

"A beautiful woman like you, ought to have a man in her life," he stated with a curious expression on his face.

"I'm dating. There's no one exclusive yet," I told him. I was flattered by his interest.

* * *

Since Terence lived in Los Angeles, we agreed on meeting at a small restaurant called Poesy's, located in Studio City. It was a convenient location for the both of us.

I entered the cozy restaurant, and the waiter directed me to a table in the mid-section area. "I'm meeting someone here," I told him.

"Yes," he nodded.

Terence was aware that I'd be wearing a figure fitting, wine tank dress, with matching high-heels. I styled my hair in flowing curls.

My eyes were riveted on the entrance, waiting for Terrence to appear. He arrived ten minutes late.

"Sorry I'm late. How are you?" Terrence asked.

I stood to give him a warm greeting. "I'm doing fine," I replied as I shook his hand.

We mirrored each other's smile as we sat down.

"So we've finally met," I eyed him.

"Yes," he grinned. "You look gorgeous and the men here look good too," he glanced around the room.

Uh-oh, down-low alert, I thought.

The waiter brought drinks. Looking over the menu I told him what I wanted.

Terrence studied the menu and then ordered.

I watched in utter disbelief as Terrence's eyes checked-out one guy after the next. One of the guys he eyed walked inside the restroom.

"Joi would you excuse me? I need to go to the little boys room." He disappeared to the restroom.

Returning with the food, the waiter placed the plates down on the table.

Momentarily glancing at my wristwatch, I slowly ate, waiting for Terrence to return.

Around half an hour later, Terrence emerged from the restroom. "Good the food is here," he said.

"It might be a little cold," I remarked.

"Food is food, cold or hot." He took a bite, his face closed as if guarding a secret.

"By the way, what's your sign?" I curiously asked.

"I'm a Leo, but I don't believe in signs," he chewed.

Thereafter, the guy he seemingly followed into the restroom came out the men's room walking oddly.

If 2+2=4, and if I'm not mistaken, it seems that my date just had public-toilet sex with a random male stranger. Eew! The nagging in the back of my mind refused to be stilled. I was born at night, but not last night.

Step 10: Be perceptive.

"This is a nice place, huh?" he smiled at me.

I nodded; wanting to run, not walk out of there.

As we were eating, coldness came over the atmosphere. I felt a disconnection. The strange twinge of disappointment made me lose my appetite. I couldn't help but think of poor Gege and what she's been through. It seemed like such a demonic situation. I ran to the ladies' room and cried.

I'm willing to love a black man, but I don't want to be hurt in return. Nowadays, most of the good ones marry white women.

If the good Lord would only remember me, I think I'd be okay.

"So have you found a man yet?" Destiny plopped down on my living room leather couch.

"Don't ask," I sighed.

"That bad huh?"

I nodded. "In my search I've found men who are either shallow, unavailable, on the down-low or gay," I pouted.

"Girl, stop acting so whipped. You have to give it time. It takes a little time, sometimes," she reassured.

"It takes time, all right." I picked up a box of assorted chocolates and offered some to Destiny, "Help yourself."

"Chocolate is my favorite temptation," she picked out a few pieces.

"It's my comfort food. I'm already on my second box," I chewed a piece of candy.

"What ya watchin'?"

"A romance flick. I wanna find love too," I whined.

"This thing you're going through is just a temporary funk. Try to think of it as a passing thing," she said in a convincing tone of voice.

"This too will pass," I agreed.

"Smile, it's good for you. Come on," she coaxed.

I cracked a smile.

"There's someone out there for you; I'm sure of it," Destiny said with optimism.

"I'll keep looking," I stated with determination. "I'm glad I have my 3-day weekend coming up. We get Monday off for the fourth of July. Yeah-yea," I basked in the thought.

"I'm so jealous, because I have to work," she pouted.

"Don't be hatin' all right. Jealousy is a negative energy."

"I thrive on positivity and love," she smirked.

"I do too. My things are free from all negativity. Why are you double talking then?" I picked at her.

"Shh, let's watch the movie," she laughed.

"All right class, this evening I'd like for you to write a poem composed entirely of questions," Ms. Sinclair told us.

Hypothetically thinking, I asked myself if Randy were to tell me that he loved me, what would be my response? I opened my journal to a blank page and began writing . . .

> Do you love me?
> Do you know who I am or what I believe?
> Do you know how I feel or what moves me?
> There's more to me than what you see.
> Do you love me?

So what, if one verse is not a question. I think I wrote a good poem, and I'm proud of it, I smiled to myself.

Writing poetry for a hobby has brought a sense of meaning to my life. I have discovered a part of me I didn't know I had before. I've had hidden talent.

An Asian student raised his hand.

"Yes," she replied.

"I've heard a lot about metaphors and similes, but what is a paradox?" he asked.

"A paradox is a contradictory statement. It pairs two direct opposites as if both could be true. Charles Dickens's famous novel *A tale of Two Cities* begins with this sentence: "It was the best of times; it was the worst of times." Isn't it a contradictory statement?"

He nodded and scribbled notes.

"A paradox simply adds contrast to figurative language. For instance, a child seems even more of a child when she sits on the lap of her grandmother."

"I know of an oxymoron statement from Shakespeare's *Romeo and Juliet*, Juliet says, "Parting is such sweet sorrow . . . .""

Ms. Sinclair nodded. "The contradictory words, "sweet sorrow," are a good example of the kind of paradox called oxymoron. A poet uses many kinds of contrast."

I took down notes as well.

"By show of hands, how many of you have written an original poem in regards to the assignment I gave you this evening?"

Hands went up all over the classroom.

"Let's here from the superstar first. Curtis what do you have for us?" Ms. Sinclair smiled at him.

He laughed. "Its short and to the point."

> If I kissed you,
> would you know
> how I feel?
> Would it give you
> a thrill,
> if I kissed you?

"I'm sure it would give whomever a thrill if you kissed her," Ms. Sinclair remarked.

The whole class laughed.

I smiled when he caught my eye. "Hi," I mouthed the word, gazing into his blue, blue eyes. Curtis fascinates me just like poetry. I wonder if he's trying to tell me something? Things that may be hard to say may be easy to write. I've been able to put my feelings into words through poetry.

Sitting at my desk in the poetry workshop, I couldn't keep myself from thinking about Curtis with forward curiosity. I allowed my subconscious thoughts to surface. I wondered if he was romantically interested in me, or if he was only trying to be nice. It could be that he was just being flirtatious, I pondered. The one thing I knew was, we had been flirting with each other like crazy; it was up to fate whether it would lead to anything more.

Chapter 7

Attempting to play the scale on my flute, I realized that I was using my time the way I've dreamed it to be used. With each passing day of practice it brought me one step closer to achieving my goal of becoming an accomplished flute artist. Each time I repeated the scale, I could hear slight improvements.

At the close of the day, I noticed a beautiful quiet sunset filtering through my living room drapes. I stood from my chair and walked across the warm hardwood floor to my window to enjoy the view. A sense of hope and perspective rushed through me. Its multicolored display had a brilliant calmness that touched my soul.

Placing the flute up to my chin, I looked skyward and made an effort to serenade the evening sky. That's when the ringing of the phone cut in. I carefully placed my flute on the coffee table and picked up the phone.

"Hello," I answered.

"I have a favor to ask," Tiffany paused.

"It depends," I replied.

"Could you be more open-minded?"

"Ah-oh. What is it?"

"I saw the woman that Max wanted me to have a threesome with and I could never do it with her. I told Max I'd feel better about having a threesome, if I chose the girl. The first person I thought of was you. I want to know who you know and touch who you touch. Joi would you do it with us please?" Tiffany begged.

"Tiffany, I honestly don't believe you. Are you serious?"

"I'm just saying I wouldn't mind having a threesome with you. Will you do it for me?" she urged. "I don't want to lose Max, I love him."

"You want me to sacrifice my virtue for Max?"

"Don't you ever wonder how it is to throw all caution to the wind?" she asked.

"No, because It's too risky. I don't do threesomes. Tiffany what has gotten into you? You don't even seem like yourself."

"Now I'm sorry I brought the whole thing up."

"Have you had too much to drink?"

"I've only had a couple of drinks. I'm okay though. Max, she's not gonna do it."

"Why not?" a male voice in the background asked.

"It's not her thing," she yelped.

"Tiff, I have to go. Bye." I hung up. I must stand against the madness.

"I hope I'll find what you two have, in a relationship of my own someday," I told my parents as we ate supper at the dining room table.

"So how has it been going so far?" Mom asked.

"I've dated Randy Kennedy, but he doesn't seem interested in us getting to know each other on a deeper level. We're not on the same page. Sex is the only thing on his mind. Whatever happened to courting?"

"There's the kind of woman that a man messes around with, and then there's the kind of woman that a man wants to keep around. I've had my share of loose women before I met your Ma."

"Spare me the gritty details," Mom sighed.

"I married a keeper. You know what I'm saying? Never be desperate or easy, that will chase a good man away," Dad told me.

"When your Dad came around trying to sweep me off my feet, I was like Fort Knox; I kept my legs securely closed. He knew that I was the kind of woman he'd have to respect to get anywhere with me."

"Men like a little challenge sometimes. Let a man be a man. Your part is to make him interested in you. Then, let him do the pursing," he advised as he chewed.

"If he's interested, he'll pursue you," Mom added.

According to my parents view on how to play this game called love, I'm not suppose to do anything but make a man interested. If he's interested, he will come. I figure they must know something, because they're still in love after 38 years of being together.

Part of a man's nature is to come, see, and conquer. They are hunters. I don't think of myself as prey. I see myself as precious loot to be found by a worthy hunter.

Step 11: Make him interested in me.

* * *

Having a taste for some apple pie, I took a walk in the warm sunshine to the local grocers, wearing a yellow sundress. While I was there I also purchased: whip cream, salmon and a bag of sweet plums. As I was exiting the market I glanced inside my grocery bag to make sure I had all my items.

"Hey good-looking!" a guy in a gold Chevrolet yelled out his window. He drove up and began to cruise beside me as I was walking home down the sidewalk.

I continued strutting along with my bag cradled in my arm acting as if I hadn't heard him.

He honked his horn.

Glancing around, I smiled at him. "Hello," I said. He looked passable.

"You can talk," he laughed. "Would you go out with a guy like me?"

"I don't know," I walked on.

"You look so good, I can't believe my eyes. I don't usually talk to women this way. I had to say something to you. Would you like to go for a ride?"

"No thank you," I replied, waiting for the stoplight to turn green.

"See you around sexy," he yelled as he sped off.

Raising my head up, a gentle breeze blew through my flowing hair and I felt amazing. Receiving that kind of attention reminded me of my teen years. I've still got it, I thought to myself with a smile.

Early morning, I had a meeting in the conference room with my team of customer service representatives. We all sat around a big oval table and discussed changes that were on the horizon at Health Gist National. Certain associates also voiced their concerns.

"Effective immediately, you must say, "Thank you for calling Health Gist National." at the end of every call," I notified.

"What if the member disconnects the line before I have a chance to close the call properly?" Nana asked.

"You would be excused in that case," I replied.

She nodded.

Looking over my memo, I said, "Points will be deducted if you say, "yeah," instead of "yes," or "nah," instead of "no," on a call. Give attention to using proper grammar. Health Gist National wants every call to be handled with professionalism."

"Ah crap!" Nikki let out a deep sigh.

"Some of you have been abusing independent time. Since some of you keep using more than fifteen minutes of independent time a day, it has been determined that independent time has now been cut down to ten minutes a day. Those of you who continue to use more than your allotted independent time will be written up."

"I've never used over fifteen minutes of independent time. Why do I have to suffer for what someone else did?" Cindy asked.

"Health Gist National already provides the required breaks and lunch periods for you. Independent time is a courtesy not a right."

"The rules are getting so stiff I can hardly breath. You can't get water from a stone! What if I get sick and need more time in the restroom?" Lamar complained.

"I didn't make these rules, but I'm sure exceptions would be made," I answered.

"Thank you," he sighed with both hands raised in the air.

I felt so mechanical while I was giving out those notifications, like a robot to be exact. I'd be irked too if I were in their shoes.

Heading down the hallway to the poetry workshop, I glanced back and spotted Curtis a few feet behind. He motioned for me to come to him. I stopped in my tracks and waited for him to catch up.

"How you doing?" Curtis greeted.

"I'm fine."

"I know that. Tell me something I don't know," he gave me a warm hug.

The mere touch of his hand sent a warming shiver through me. I savored the moment in my mind. "So how are you?" I asked.

"Oh I'm phenomenal," he smiled.

His smile made me feel so happy inside. I managed a tentative smile in return. I could sense a connection, a kindling deep within. Curtis and I walked into the class together as if we were a couple. We sat next to each other.

Ms. Sinclair wrote notes on the board. "There's a poetry form that originated in India, called the Naani. It consists of 4 lines. The total lines contain 20 to 25 syllables. The following is an example of a Naani."

> Romantic love is
> looking for me.
> Around some winding
> road we'll find each other.

After I wrote a Naani, I knew that poetry would remain an important part of my life long after the workshop.

> Love was a mysterious
> stranger, who became
> my closest friend,
> since I've known you.

"Have you written one?" Curtis asked.
"Yes," I replied.
"Show me yours and I'll show you mines," he smiled.
We traded journals.

> Love's anatomy
> between you and me.
> I'm loving your face your mind.
> If you want me show me a sign.

After I read the poem, somehow I knew that Curtis had addressed it to me. He was letting me know in no subtle way, that I had attracted his attention. He's looking at me with so much interest. He's nibbling on my bait. Now, all I have to do is catch him.

"Nicely done. Your Naani reminds me of a note from the inside of a greeting card. I like it," Curtis told me as he handed my journal back to me.

"Thank you. I like your poetry too. I'm into the anatomy of love," I smiled at him.

"Poetry is so intimate. It's filled with feelings," he told me.

"Yes it is," I replied as I handed him his journal.

"I'm glad I'm getting to know you better," his gaze met mines.

"Same here," I smiled into his eyes.

It seems I was getting close to Curtis through poetry. I loved being able to see him more than once a week. I wanted to find out more about him. I couldn't help wondering what sort of person he was, where he was from, where he lives, what he eats, his likes and dislikes. I'd like to discover the real person beneath his superstar image . . . . He seemed decent enough, if I were any judge of character.

A pupil raised her hand.

Ms. Sinclair nodded.

"My name is Pratiti and I have a Naani to share. I'm Asian Indian. Thank you for teaching us about a poetry form that's from my native land. Here's my Naani . . ."

> Paper faces,
> thinking one thing,
> saying another, hiding
> what's beneath the surface.

"Very interesting Naani," Ms. Sinclair clapped.

The class applauded.

"Anyone else?" the instructor scanned the room.

A few other students recited their poems.

Analyzing my feelings for Curtis, I came to the conclusion that it was more than infatuation. I've admired him in the past. But now my affection for him had somehow deepened.

I wished Curtis were mine, and then I felt guilty for wanting a man who's engaged to be married. A thought of Curtis making love to Crystal flashed through the corridors of my mind and I became nauseous. I looked over at Curtis with wishful eyes, and for a moment his face reminded me of an angel. My whole being seemed filled with waiting. "Oh God, I think I love him," I whispered to myself.

The English word "love" has been so overused that it has lost its true meaning. The anatomy of love is more than sex. It's love for the mind body and soul. There are a number of Greek words for love: eros, philia, and agape, just to name a few. I figure my ideal love would have a combination of the three in his heart for me.

Eros type of love is romantic, as well as passionately erotic. Eros is based on our perceptions of what's sensually stimulating or desirable. Eros vanishes when a situation is interpreted as undesirable.

Philia kind of love is shared in friendships. Close friends share common interests, ideals experiences and activities.

Agape love seeks the other's well being; it's patient and kind. It does not behave rudely. Agape is not just a feeling; it's an action, agapeo. This form of love endures the test. Eros and philia can thrive in agape's ambiance.

If I ever tell a man that I love him, I'll have the three in mind.

The kind of love I'm looking for is more than physical, which is eros. It's even more than philia, which is mental. I also need a man who will love me with a spiritual kind of love, agape.

When it comes to good old fashion love, I've got that. I've got enough love to warm up a cold heart.

I'm the whole package. I'm not trying to give the man I love a package of damaged goods. I care about myself and there is no sin in that. I must also keep in mind that I'm a virtuous woman.

Step 12: Choose a man who sincerely loves me with eros, philia, and agape love.

Chapter 8

Health Gist National had a few job openings, so I was called on to interview a few perspective associates.

"How did you hear about us?" I asked.

"A friend of mine told me that you were hiring," Elaine McKenzie answered nervously.

"How long have you been looking for work? Your resume showed a lapse in your work history."

"After I was laid-off from my last job, I took some time out to examine my career goals and where I was going with my life. I've just begun my search in the last few weeks. I want to like my job, so I've been selective about the positions I consider. Your company and this position are of great interest to me."

"I've gathered from your answer that you are familiar with Health Gist National and what it provides," I smiled warmly.

"Yes, I went to the Health Gist National's Website and did some research on your company. I was impressed, so I seized the opportunity and applied for the Customer Service Representative position."

"Why do you want this job?"

"When I saw the job posting I knew I had found what I was looking for. I have a strong customer service work history, so I have the experience and knowledge needed to communicate and build customer relationships. I think I'm a perfect match for this position. I have what you need, and you have what I want," Elaine eloquently concluded.

"Elaine, I must say, you have sold yourself. I'm going to ask the Human Resource Department to hire you in time for the next training class. There will be a background check and drug testing. If all is clear, I'll see you in the call center in the near future," I stood up from my office chair and offered a handshake.

"Thank you Ms. Glamier," she chimed with a smile from ear to ear.

"I'll have the Human Resource Department email an offer letter to you; it will include the starting salary amount. You'll have it in writing shortly."

"Hot damn," she laughed.

"FYI, profanity is not allowed in the call center."

"Excuse me," she chirped.

"You're excused," I gave a polite nod.

That evening I made a quick dash to Shoney's Shoes. Destiny told me that men found women in heels irresistible. I'm not one who knocks good advice, so I bought a pair of sexy silver stilettos that were actually comfortable. I also found a cute black miniskirt at the store next door.

Step 13: Be alluring in high-heels.

*   *   *

The bell over the front entrance sounded as I opened and closed the door of Flute & Voice Info. I walked inside to wait until it was time for my flute lesson. I caught a glimpse of Curtis frolicking with his dark and lovely Crystal. They were huddled up kissing in his office.

My heart dropped. "Curtis should be kissing me like that, not her," I muttered to myself. Tears welled up in my eyes. It was a knee-jerk reaction. I couldn't help it. It hurt to see him kissing someone else. I know I didn't have a right to feel that way, but I did.

Curtis looked my way and his eyes locked with mines.

Quickly, I turned and walked away out of his view. Swiping at a wayward tear, I gazed out the front window and watched the traffic of the busy street.

Approximately four minutes later the two of them came out the office giggling.

Pulling a chair, I took a seat and assembled my flute.

"Curtis, your next pupil's lesson doesn't start till another five minutes," Crystal whined as she glanced at her wristwatch.

"I'm waiting for my lesson Ma'am," I told her.

"Where does she get off calling me Ma'am?" she huffed. "My name is Crystal," she rolled her eyes.

"Hey, I didn't mean anything by it. I suppose you would prefer to be called bitch instead," I eyed her.

She laughed.

"Whoa, lightin' up baby. She's my student," Curtis massaged her puny shoulders.

"Alright love," she gave him a peck on the lips. "Don't forget our plans for tonight," Crystal told him as she headed for the exit.

"What plans?" He looked puzzled.

"You know," she chimed.

"She was so rude," I said, after she left. "I treat others the way I'd want to be treated."

"That's a good philosophy. I apologize for her bad attitude."

"Thank you," I sighed.

Step 14: Don't be a bitch like Crystal.

"Alright Joi, what are the two ways to change the sounds we make on the flute?" Curtis asked as he ran his fingers through his slightly wavy golden blond hair.

"Uh, with the keys and by the way we blow into the flute," I answered.

"So you have been listening to me," he smiled. "You're correct. Between those two things we can play all forty notes," he instructed.

Tiffany seemed upset. She wanted to go outside to get some air. We were quiet for several moments as we walked down the sidewalk during our lunchtime.

"Max broke it off with me. I even had the threesome with him. I feel so used," Tiffany mournfully confessed.

"The first time I met him he squeezed my ass right under your nose. Like you said, that was Max being Max."

"I thought he would keep me around if I did what he wanted," she cried.

"Whores seldom play for keeps," I shook my head. "You're better off without him."

"Yes," she agreed. "It was a toxic relationship. He wasn't good for me anyway," a tear fell from her cheek. "But how do I get Max out of my heart?"

"You must look deep inside to find the strength to let him go and move on," I placed my hand on her shoulder.

"I know," she sobbed.

Looking out my window at the night sky, I tried to make sense of it all. I'd like to understand how to relate to men better, so when I actually get a man we'll have a chance at making it work. Sex, isn't necessarily the way to keep a man; Tiffany is proof of that. I need to dig a little deeper. What do men want besides sex? It's a given that a man wants his woman to look incredible, but what else? . . .

Step 15: Figure out what guys want.

Men don't like nagging women. My Aunt Berta once told me that she'll never forgive herself for running off Uncle Ned. She used to nag him day and night. There's a way to talk to someone and nagging is not the way.

Uncle Ned wasn't a bad man. He was a family man who also was a good provider. I miss those family get-togethers they used to have. He sure knew how to cook some good barbeque ribs.

Now poor Aunt Berta is stuck with a bum. The new guy she's with doesn't even carry his own weight when it comes to financial responsibilities.

I've learned from experience that a man likes for a woman to build him up, not tear him down. Whenever I pay Curtis a compliment, he seems to stand taller. Men like their ego stroked from time to time. I suppose women want the same thing. I'd like a man who makes me feel good about myself.

From observance, I've come to the conclusion that men are drawn to women who are open and confident. My shy to outgoing venture seems to be going well. I'd like to be with the kind of man who'd make me forget that I'm shy. I'd also like to look the man I love in the eyes and have an intimate conversation with him. I'd let him know that I'll love him and treat him right.

Wouldn't love be easy if it was like some classic romantic movie where everything works out by the end of the show? I don't know how it's going to turn out.

I held my shoulders back and my head up as I walked down the hallway like a confident woman who believed in herself. I was wearing a yellow tank top with a figure fitting black miniskirt. I swung my dark flowing curls to my back as I entered the classroom. Curtis was already seated. I gave him a polite nod and sat at a desk to the right of the room.

Curtis collected his things and crossed over to sit at the desk in back of mines. I could feel his eyes on me. "Hi," he greeted.

"Hello," I chirped. I took my compact mirror out and glided on some burgundy brew lipstick.

"I'd like to say it has been a pleasure to instruct such a poetically inclined class. Since this is the last day of the poetry workshop, I'd like to hear an original poem from each one of you, in the style of your choice," Ms. Sinclair voiced, standing in front of the class.

Thumbing through the pages of my journal, I selected an original poem to share with the class.

Curtis peeked over my shoulder at the page I opened my journal to.

> Under the sun
> I love you
> with my eyes.
> Under the moon
> I hold you
> in my heart.

"I wish I was that guy," he told me.

"Which guy?" I replied.

"Whomever you wrote that poem about," Curtis said in a serious tone of voice.

"I didn't write this poem about anyone in particular. Sometimes I write poetry about the way I'd like to experience love," I answered with my head slightly turned in his direction.

"You have a beautiful mind," he breathed.

"Thanks," I smiled. "It was just my imagination, running away with me," I sang softly.

"You have a sweet sounding voice. Crystal can't sing her way out of a bucket."

My becoming more interesting has definitely helped, I thought.

"Joi, you beautiful sexy female, I want you. I'd do anything for you. I'd give up my fiancé for you. I'd even give you free flute lessons," he voiced at low volume.

When Curtis started whispering to me from behind, I froze . . . .

Crystal isn't so hot. Her looks are lacking. There's nothing wrong with him wanting me. He's not married yet, I reasoned within myself.

"To celebrate our last day of the poetry workshop, how would you like to go out with me to a poetry cafe? Dinner would be my treat," he invited.

I turned sideways at my desk to make my response less awkward. "I don't like the love triangle situation, but if there's no strings attached, I accept."

"No strings attached. We won't even call it a date, just celebrating. I'll pick you up tomorrow at 6:00 p.m.," he smiled.

My mind was too occupied with thinking about Curtis to focus on the poetry that was being recited. It's a muffled blur. Everyone in the class read their poems, except for Curtis and me.

Although the poetry workshop was over, it left a lasting impression on me. I became a poet during the workshop. There's a verse in the Bible which inspired me, from Habakkuk 2:2. It reads, "Write the vision and make it plain on the tablets . . ." I write poetry from visions of love in my head.

Visions of Curtis flashed through my mind that whole night through.

Chapter 9

The moment Curtis and I walked inside Poetry & Roses Cafe, we were escorted to an open table. The friendly waitress took our orders quickly.

"Tonight's open mic night," Curtis smiled at me with his compelling blue eyes.

"I'd like to hear some poetic flavas," I said with anticipation.

"I've heard some good ones here," he nodded a knowing smile.

"I'm going to miss the poetry workshop," I pouted.

"Me too," he eyed me.

"Enjoy your food," the waitress placed the food and drinks on the table.

"I will," he sipped his drink.

"Thank you," I nodded.

"It's open mic night here at the Poetry & Roses Cafe," the announcer began. "First up, I'd like to welcome Curtis Cooper to the stage. Let's give it up for him!"

Applause broke out. I clapped along with the eager audience.

Curtis stepped up to the microphone and began to recite verse in the spotlight. His talk-radio sounding voice brought calm to the audience. While he recited sweet words our eyes met.

> I see your beauty
> shinning like
> the sun.
> Like an exquisite
> work of art your
> face enamors my
> heart.
> Statuesque model
> touch my life.

"Thank you," he ended.

The audience warmly applauded as he walked off the stage back to our table.

"That poem was incredible. I liked it," I beamed.

"Thanks. I was thinking of you when I wrote it," he stared at me with a longing expression.

A vaguely sensuous light passed between us. I felt myself blushing. Shut to it, words were not said. He seemed to study my face. What did he see? I wondered. Did he see that I'm the one he should love?

"It seems like you don't realize how beautiful you are," he gazed into my nut-brown eyes.

"I realize it enough."

He reached under the table and rubbed my thigh.

"I find you attractive, but could you slow down a little?" I asked him.

"Pardon me. Bad hand, bad hand," he jokingly scolded the hand that he fondled my thigh with.

"What's your favorite poetry form that we learned during the poetry workshop?" I asked.

"I'd have to say, the Rondelet. I'm going to do more," he replied.

"Love to do that," I smiled.

We listened to a few more aspiring poets, and then we called it a night.

Under the twilight starry sky Curtis walked me to my front door.

"I really had a good time," I sparkled.

"Let's do it again sometime." He kissed me ever so gently on the lips. "Have a good night." Curtis looked at me and paused for a moment before he walked back to his black Infinity.

"Good night," I waved. I stood there, watching after him. I put a finger on the soft, warm place on my lips where he had kissed me. I knew that a slender delicate thread began to form between us.

I wrote a poem called, "This Romantic Night" that evening.

> This romantic
> night,
> tasted like a
> spice of
> life.
> This romantic
> night,
> I kissed a
> star and danced
> around my room by
> moonlight.

Sunlight shined a warm glow through the parted yellow curtains, which cascaded over my bedroom window. Awakened by my alarm clock, I lay in bed for a moment and stretched. Getting up from bed, I headed for my bathroom down the hall, and then I brushed my teeth and washed my face.

Still debating on whether I should perm my wavy hair or not, I played around with my hair a bit. Before, I'd usually pull my hair back in a tight ponytail. Now that's not enough, I thought. I decided right then and there to toss the Kidee perm and keep my new hair stylist, Kiki.

"Curtis thinks I'm beautiful," I told myself as I looked at my image in the mirror. Smiling, I rubbed an eyebrow with my index finger. If he's my fate, he's mine to take, I thought.

Chapter 10

While I was on my way home form work, I happened to notice a white pickup truck with tinted windows tailgating my car. I made a right turn and the truck followed close behind. Then I made a left turn at the next street light and the unidentified person who was following me did the same. I decided that it would be best for me not to drive home, so I went to a supermarket and parked in the parking lot to wait for a while.

Moments later, I glanced around and saw Randy approaching my silver BMW. It was a surprise to see him show up out of the blue like that. It had been nearly five weeks since I last heard from him. He had on a red polo shirt and a pair of tight indigo jeans. Randy looked awesome; his innately captivating presence arrested my attention. He opened my car door, jumped into my vehicle and sat on the passenger seat.

"You drive crazy. What's up with you?" he gripped.

"Are you the one who was following me?" I asked him.

"So," he replied with a cocky disposition.

"Why are you giving me this attitude?"

"I didn't mean to. Joi, I wanted to say I'm sorry for the things I said to you before, even though it may have been true," he smirked.

"Was that an apology?"

"Time out," he cried.

"Randy, please don't have a melt-down in my car."

He laughed. "If you weren't so damn stuck-up, maybe we could get somewhere."

"Excuse me!"

"Stop fighting me woman. I don't want to fight with you, I want to make love to you."

"Oh really?"

"Shit. I miss you. I can't get you off my mind," he sighed.

"Alright, so let's start over again. How have you been?"

"Okay," he nodded. "And you?"

"I'm making it."

"What I'd like to understand is why are we apart? I know you're into me, and I'm definitely into you."

"How do you know I'm into you?" I smiled at him.

"I can see it in your eyes. You sparkle when you look at me."

"Let me grab my sunglasses," I playfully reached for them.

"Can you be serious for a minute? Don't hide your feelings from me. You should be my woman," he eyed me.

"Randy, I wanted to give us a chance. I wanted for us to get to know each other better."

"I know all I wanna know about you," his gaze moved over my body.

"I want us to be on the same page when it comes to expectations. I'd only have sex with a man who I'm in a long-term committed relationship with. When I do have sex, I'd like for it to be special, not casual. And another thing, I'd like to be in love, not just in-heat," I opened up.

"Damn! Girl, you drive a hard bargain," he sighed. "Alright, okay, oh yeah," he raised his hands in surrender.

"Are you alright with it?" I looked at him.

"I said alright didn't I?"

"You look handsome today," I complimented him.

"I know you like this," he beat his fist on his chest. "Oh it almost slept my mind. Rapalicious is coming to a Summerfest near you. We're going to do-it-to-it Saturday after next from 4:30 to 5:00. You need to be there," he announced.

"I'll be there."

"If you do a no-show, I'll camp on your doorstep."

"I'd come through rain sleet or snow to be there for you baby," I placed my hand on his knee.

Randy's lips quickly swooped in and captured mines.

I felt transported on a soft wispy cloud. It took a moment for me to come down to earth. His tantalizing smell of aftershave tempted my senses. "Ah, you naughty man you. You stole a kiss."

"To take the stolen kiss back, you must kiss me again," he raised his eyebrows repeatedly in a playful mood.

"Let's hear what you've got," Curtis waited.

Taking in a deep breath, I played the melody, "Poets and Pigs." I managed to play the whole piece without making one mistake, a note worthy accomplishment.

"Excellent," he clapped. "Tell you what, there's going to be a recital held for my students. Would you like to participate?"

"Yes, but have you ever had to deal with stage fright before?" I asked.

"Nervous jitters are a natural part of entertaining. Don't let it keep you from performing," he encouraged. "You need to know the musical piece well and feel comfortable presenting it. Practice every day to gain the confidence you need to manage your stress about performing."

I nodded.

"You also can use breathing exercises to control your anxiety. Practice by inhaling through your nose for two seconds. Then exhale through your mouth for four seconds. Do this breathing exercise right before your performance to calm your nerves. If you get nervous during the performance, close your eyes for a second and imagine the audience's happy faces. It works for me," he gave a knowing smile.

"Alright," I held on to every word.

"Then we're all set," he clapped his hands together once.

"You're amazing, you know that?" I gazed at him in awe.

"I hope I'm all you think I am," he inhaled and exhaled.

"I'm sure you are," I smiled.

"The recital will be held at the Fairington Auditorium, this Friday evening at 6:00 sharp. I'm going to put you on the program."

"I hope I rise to the occasion," I said with a twinge of anxiety.

"Oh, you'll do great," Curtis supported.

*   *   *

The buy-me scent of new cloths always makes me feel a little happy inside. Tiffany and I combed through the mall.

"I need an exquisite dress to wear to my flute recital," I told Tiffany.

"If you need something upscale to wear, we can go to Elite Pleasures."

"Where is it?" I glanced around the mall.

"Down there to the right," she pointed.

We made our way through the crowd.

Looking through the storefront window, I spotted thee dress. "That's hot," I exclaimed. "I like that silver metallic dress." I walked inside the store.

"Joi, your taste has become sexy and smooth. I'm liking the new you," she smiled.

"Well I needed to be more bold to get the right man's attention."

"How's your man search coming along?"

"I'm trying to figure out who's Mr. Right."

"From my track record I sure wouldn't know," she shook her head.

"I love that black necklace, I'm going to buy it," I told her.

Tiffany held up a shimmering lilac blouse. "Sweet."

"Lilac is your color," I nodded.

"I'm sure you'll rock that dress."

We stood in front of a large full-length three-panel mirror checking out our selections.

"I've been thinking about learning how to play an instrument too," Tiffany told me in an as-a matter-of-fact tone of voice.

"Trying to become more cultured are we? Which instrument do you have in mind?"

"The piano. I'd like to have an interest in something that won't break my heart, for a change."

"Good for you."

"I'm also going to start coming to church too," she pouted.

"The doors of the church are open," I gave a good-natured smile and placed my arm around her shoulders.

When we arrived at Club Improvise, the guy at the entrance told Tiffany and I to come in as soon as he spotted us in line.

"He must think we're hot. Huh oh, I love VIP treatment," Tiffany giggled.

The waiter showed us to a table and took our orders.

"I'll have the pink salmon dish, garlic bread and the salad please," I requested.

"Um, I'll have the shrimp, with the side order," Tiffany selected from the menu.

He returned and poured each of us a complimentary glass of wine. We sipped on our drinks while we waited for our food.

"I've been eating less since Max and I broke up. I think it's because I've been so depressed. Lately, I've been spending a lot of time at the gym. Evidently it's paid off. It's been years since I've received VIP treatment," she smiled.

"I'm glad you're getting over him," I gave a half smile.

"Here's to meeting new people," Tiffany proposed a toast.

"Yes," I sipped my drink.

"Ah, I love this place," she sighed. "I felt like going somewhere to unwind. Thanks for being the one who invited me out this time," she squeezed my hand.

"Friends help each other out," I said in a cheerful tone of voice.

"You're a good friend."

I gave her a smile from my heart.

"I can't get over the change in you. You've opened up like a flower. And you've got this sexy aura now that's out of this world," she eyed me.

"I had to break out of my shell and let some eligible bachelors know I'm available."

"You said you weren't sure about someone?" Tiffany questioned.

"I'm in the valley of decision. I'm seeing two guys, but I'm not sure about either of them yet."

"You go girl!" she laughed.

"I'm not fucking them. We're just talking and kissing," I added.

"That's still a big step for you," she nodded.

"I believe in getting emotionally in touch, before physical."

"I ain't mad at ya," she smiled. "Maybe I should have done that," she looked at her wine glass as if she were in deep thought.

"It's my revolution baby," I said in a singsong tone of voice and sipped some wine.

"It's your thing. Do you."

The waiter placed our food on the table.

"Thanks," I looked up and then a tipsy feeling came over me. I took a bite of food to absorb some of the alcohol. "Delicious," I commented.

Tiffany gave an approving nod.

"I bet you're giving those two guys blue-balls," she giggled.

"What?"

"It's when a man is about to . . ."

"I get it, never mind the vivid explanation. White girl, you know you make 'em trip too."

"Max took my confidence, but I think I'm getting some of it back. Wow, look at him," she eyed a handsome Italian looking guy.

I leaned forward to see him better through the dim light. "Tiff, from where I'm sitting he looks kind of fine."

"True that. But look, he's with her," she scowled.

"Oh."

"I ran out of gas the other day. I hate buying it, because the price of gasoline is too high," she frowned. "This cute guy helped me out though," she perked up.

"I feel the same way you do about it, but setting yourself up to be stranded out in the middle of nowhere is not a solution either."

"We have to pay nearly $5.00 a gallon for gasoline, and it seems like no one in the government gives a damn about it. Filling up my tires with air is not helping at all," she complained.

"There ought to be a law. You know how some apartments have rent control. There ought to be gas price control. We should never be charged more than $3.00 a gallon for gas," I told her.

"Yeah. There should be a limit on how much we're to be charged for gas."

"The United States of America needs to become energy independent. We need a President who cares about everyday people."

"That's right," she nodded.

"It would help businesses if gas prices were lower. The unemployment rate has skyrocketed. America doesn't have enough jobs for it's own citizens, because illegal immigrants are taking jobs. Businesses are leaving and outsourcing jobs offshore. California is bankrupt. The whole country is nearly bankrupt, while money is being wasted on ridiculous earmarks. The government needs to stop all the wasteful spending and think up innovative ways to help our nation."

"What's happening to our country?" Tiffany whined.

"We need a government for the people, by the people and of the people, that's what."

"Who's for the people?"

"I don't know. Currently, there's no one on the scene that is trying to fix these problems. So many politicians have their own agenda."

"I'm tired of talking about politics," she sighed.

"Ooh, that's my song." The music made me feel like dancing, so I went for it. I strutted to the dance floor like Tiffany would do and danced like no one was watching.

While I was walking the plush burgundy carpeted floor of the call center I heard Josh, one of the representatives in my department cheer, "Compliment call!"

"Transfer the call to my extension. I'll pick it up," I told him. Rushing back to my office, I picked up the receiver on the first ring.

"Yes," I answered.

"Hello, are you Josh's supervisor?"

"I'm his supervisor."

"Josh has been so helpful. I called twice before about the same issue to no avail. I'm so glad I got Josh when I called today, he's been like an angel of mercy."

"Oh really?"

"Oh gosh yes. The others wouldn't let me finish explaining my situation. They said the soonest my transfer could be effective was next month. I knew that couldn't be right. See I recently moved out of the area and needed another PCP in my new area. Josh found that my transfer to Dr. Givens could be effective right away. He even explained how my HMO plan worked."

"Josh will be recognized for doing a good job."

"I think he deserves a raise," she recommended.

"May I ask your name?"

"Of course, my name is Linzy Holloway."

"All right Ms. Holloway. My name is Joi Glamier and thank you so much for calling Health Gist National. Have a good day."

"Thanks so much."

"Happy 39th Wedding Anniversary!" I shouted and presented my parents with a bouquet of orange blossoms, which symbolizes eternal love.

"Are those for me?" Mom smiled.

"Yes, these are for you. Here's your card," I offered.

They read the card in unison.

"I'd like to sing a song for you two, to celebrate your happy anniversary." I sung a classic wedding song, "You And I."

"Joi, thank you for everything. I love the flowers. You sung beautifully," she gave me a hug.

My Dad wiped his eyes with a handkerchief, "Girl, you've done sung me happy," he sniffled.

"Ah," I said.

"I think he's become more sentimental," Mom said.

"Thanks sweets," he told me with a cheerful smile on his face.

"You're welcome." As I stood in my Mom and Dad's living room I knew there would always be a vision in my heart of the way love should be, and I felt even more determined to not settle for anything less.

Chapter 11

A light breeze rustled through the line of palm trees on both sides of the boulevard inspiring the leaves to dance.

Looking in the rearview mirror, I ran my fingers through my stylish hair. Then I stepped out of my silver BMW in the cool of the evening, wearing an exquisite silver metallic dress, with matching high-heels. My hair was styled in an elegant updo.

Collecting my flute and purse, I locked my car door and started towards the Fairington Auditorium. Curtis and Crystal were walking up the sidewalk from the opposite direction. Nearing the entrance of the auditorium, I paused for a moment. "Hi you two," I gritted a smile.

"Hi. Ready to perform?" Curtis asked in a business tone of voice.

"I'm ready as I'll ever be," I gave a half smile.

He exchanged a quick smile with me.

Crystal eyed her wristwatch. "We don't want to be late, Boo," she snubbed.

Choosing to not let her get me down, I ordered my thoughts to positive things, like how dreamy Curtis looked in his sage designer shirt and brown slacks.

The two of them made their entrance after me. They managed to find a couple of seats near the front. I sat a few rows behind them. As the recital began, I gazed at Curtis and Crystal with an unconcealed stare. Resentment crept in when I began to feel like I was playing second fiddle to her.

Curtis glanced back at me a few times during the program. I focused my eyes on the recital with the intention of keeping a calm mood.

When my turn came to play my musical piece, I headed up the aisle to the stage trying to remember the tips Curtis gave me about performing. For a moment I felt like I was about to hyperventilate while I was inhaling and exhaling. Then I calmed down. I went up the stairs to the stage and played a short rendition of "Poets and Pigs." To cure my jitters, I played the whole piece with my eyes closed and pictured the audience's smiling faces.

The audience gave me a satisfied round of applause. Curtis looked pleased. I'm hoping this will be the first of many events I share with him.

After the recital I got the notion that Curtis wasn't ready to give up Crystal. All at once I felt so much anxiety. I began to feel leery about dating him.

In a situation like this, Curtis would have to make it perfectly clear to Crystal that he doesn't want her anymore. If he won't do that, I'll know he's trying to play games with my heart and I'll forget about having a romantic relationship with him. If he doesn't breakup with her, she'll be lurking in the shadows otherwise.

I have no idea how Curtis views me. Does he see me as a keeper? He might be trying to play me. I'm not going to be blindsided by some shit. Maybe he's acting like he'd give up Crystal to trick me into letting him get some.

My Grandma Ocum was full of spiritual truths. She once told me, "Soul ties are formed through sexual relations. Through sex, lovers souls become knit together. These soul ties affect the soul, mind, will and emotions. Sex is a natural course of nature. The times of coming together should be like a celebration. The one you mate determines your fate. Don't sell yourself short, wait for a decent man who'll marry you. Keep holding yourself up." Those were the last words she told me before she went up to Glory.

I know there are soul ties involved between Curtis and Crystal. I hate the thought of their souls being intertwined together. I never asked Grandma whether soul ties could be reversed or broken. I suppose that soul ties can only be undone by God. David, the Psalmist, once wrote of his soul being restored. I guess I'll say a prayer for Curtis.

Social influences compel us to give it up, to get a man. But, will giving it up guarantee the desired outcome? Tiffany's mistake reminds me of what not to do. She gave up her milk and cookies way too soon.

I've been a firm believer in the metaphoric expression, "Why buy the cow when you can get the milk free?" It is a fact that there have been less marriages occurring since a majority of people feel that they would rather test the waters by living together first. They used to call it, "Living in sin."

Nowadays, men have been spoiled by an abundant supply of free milk. Would a man like that be ready for a woman like me?

Before I worked at Health Gist National, I was a Customer Service Agent for Burgham Collectibles.

Often, the manufacture would make limited editions of certain "collectibles." Limited editions were always considered as more desirable or valuable than mass productions. Serious collectors happily paid extreme prices for products that were in limited supply.

If human nature is the same in regards to relationships, there should be some men out there who'll appreciate a woman like me. I'm a limited edition. I'm the kind of woman a good man would want to keep, not use and discard. I'm not a fly-by-night piece of ass. I'm a valuable person who's worth the wait. If a man really loves me, he'll wait for me.

I'm not saying that a man or a woman should be someone's all in all. I'm never going to depend on any man to be the sole provider of my happiness. I've found a considerable amount of happiness within myself. There are other things in life that makes me happy, like playing the flute, writing poetry, hanging out with friends, me-time etcetera. But, I still would like to experience true love.

"We're up next," Randy said as they were unloading the sound equipment from the brown van to the stage.

"Hi Randy," I gave a warm smile and waved.

"Hi beautiful," he gave a heart-warming smile.

"She looks better than your old girlfriend, Gwen," one of the band members remarked.

"Joi, this is Lonnie, he plays the keyboard. Nait plays the rhythm guitar, and Vincent plays the base. Dexter sings and raps. As you know I play the drums. Together we are Rapalicious," Randy introduced with a wave of his arm.

"Hey," I waved.

"Hi Joi," the band greeted in unison.

"Look at you in your hot-pink capri set, looking fine," Nait complimented me.

"She's with me," Randy told him in a-hands-off tone of voice.

Rapalicious took their position on stage. The atmosphere was electric. The stout announcer introduced them, and then all systems were go. The band performed like they did that sort of thing everyday. The crowd was drawn to the great sounding music they made. I was truly impressed by Rapalicious.

Randy looked super-hot that day. He played the drums with so much spirit and energy; I could feel the beat.

"I've got one. How is a heart like a musician?" I asked.

"You tell me," Randy replied.

"They both have a beat," I gave the punch line.

"Not bad," he nodded.

"Here's one," Dexter started, "How do you make a bandstand?"

"How?" Randy asked.

"Take away their chairs," he chuckled.

I giggled.

"Who looks the finest, Randy or me?" Dexter asked me.

"Randy looks the best and I don't want to hear another word about it."

"He paid her to say that," Dexter mouthed-off.

"Don't be hatin' Poindexter," Randy took a bite off his barbeque chicken leg.

"Thanks for inviting us over for dinner Joi," Nait said.

"You're welcome." I ate a bite of wild rice.

I found it relaxing to entertain guests. We were all seated around my dining room table enjoying a home cooked meal. It was interesting being a part of male chitchat. All that male testosterone in the room kind of turned me on.

"The carrot salad is good. I like the raisins in it," Randy chewed.

"You ought to taste my coleslaw. It's a tasty way to eat something good for you," I told him.

"Baby, you're good for me. I might want to make you my wife," Randy gave me the eye.

"Ooh," the band members cooed at Randy.

"Ah shut up," he told them.

"Do you mind if I smoke?" Lonnie took out a box of cigarettes.

"I don't have any ashtrays, so what does that tell ya?" I smirked.

"Ha ha, she's funny," Randy laughed.

"Yeah, that was funny," Nait agreed and chuckled. "So what's cracking between you and my boy, Randy?"

"We're trying to find love," I stared at the fizzing bubbles in my wine glass.

"I hope you find it soon, because he's about to explode," Lonnie pressured.

"I'm not looking to just get laid. I want a meaningful relationship," I told them.

"Sexy, I'm tired of being alone," Randy put his hand on my check.

"He's looking for a home. Take him in, please," Lonnie laughed.

"Don't you know light skinned brothas are back in style?" Randy flirted with his eyes.

"Vincent, you are so quiet," I tried to change the subject.

He winked at me.

"Rapalicious, you are good," I affirmed. "Here's to Rapalicious," I proposed a toast and sipped my drink.

"We made it happen," Dexter nodded.

Liking Curtis and Randy is like having two favorite flavors of ice cream. Right now I don't know which one I like better, vanilla or butterscotch. I like both of them.

> Just the three of us.
> I look forward to
> seeing
> your faces.
> I can only
> be with one.
> Who will it be?

Whoever I choose will be like my favorite pair of shoes. I must choose the right one or I'll lose. The moon will make me know, hasten quickly show . . .

Chapter 12

While crossing the street to the computerized planetarium theater, the light breeze grew colder. Curtis slid a masculine arm around my waist, sending a warm loving sensation through my entire body.

When the lights at the planetarium were turned off, a digital projector filled the huge dome shaped ceiling with visions that looked like the night sky, full of stars. The narrator pointed out and named major stars, planets and constellations.

"Venus is the brightest planet and the third brightest object in the sky. Because of its appearance at sunrise and sunset, the ancient Greeks thought it was two different planets, and gave it different names, Phosphorous, light bringer, morning star, and Hesperus, the evening star. Our name for the planet is the mythological goddess's Roman name," the narrator explained.

"Venus is associated with sexual desire. The symbol for Venus is a stylized mirror, as befits the goddess of love and beauty. It is also the commonly used symbol for woman, or the female sex," he added.

"Neptune is said to be the higher octave of Venus. Neptune lay in the depths of space. Very little was known about this planet until the

Voyager 2, space probe flew by it in 1989. Neptune symbolizes inspiration, dreams, illusion, intuition and spiritual enlightenment."

"Neptune also has a faint series of rings around it, but it is not visible from Earth. Neptune's orbit is almost perfectly circular; only Venus has a more circular orbit."

Other couples and families were observing the sights.

"Astronomy is so romantic," I breathed in awe.

Curtis placed his arm around my waist and began to massage my stomach.

I thought that was strange. I didn't know if he was horny or what. Maybe it was the way we were cozied up in a dark room.

Curtis looked up at the magnificent display as he continued massaging me.

My heart was beating so fast from being close to him. I was starting to feel a little freaky myself. I wanted to give him a warm response, so he would know that I was interested. Through my bashfulness I managed to place my arm around his strong firm waistline. It was a euphoric moment for me.

Afterwards, Curtis took me to a romantic restaurant in Glendale, California. I'll never forget that night; "Funkytown" was blasting on his car stereo. The city lights were so enchanting; I soaked in the scenery.

Newyork's was exquisite and the food was delectable.

"I find music as pleasurable as sex. Music takes me away to another place. It's like an escape," Curtis stated.

"I know what you mean. I'm a lover of the arts as well," I nodded.

"If it wasn't for the music, I don't know what I'd do sometimes," he sighed.

"Whenever I hear a song that I really like, I find myself getting lost in the music. It's like taking a mini vacation," I related.

"Only a true music lover would understand," he smiled.

"I see music is a very important part of your life."

"Indeed it is," he sipped from his wine glass.

"Do you still have concerts sometimes?"

"From time to time. I still love to sing. It's one of those innate things."

"I'd love for you to make another CD," I told him with sheer enthusiasm.

"Maybe I will," he rested his hand atop mines. "Crystal told me that my singing sensation days are over."

"Why is she so anal?"

"That's Crystal."

"An artist that is talented as you are could make a successful come back," I told him.

"I'm glad you believe in me. I still write and produce songs for the music industry. The royalties aren't bad."

I nodded with interest.

Step 16: I will be supportive and not a roadblock like Crystal.

"Let's hear about you. Where were you born?" His eyes were filled with a curious deep longing.

"I was born in Valley Village, California."

"So you live in your nest area."

"Where were you born?" I asked.

"In New York City. I moved to California to stay out of trouble and start my own business, Flute & Voice Info. I needed a new scene," he ran his fingers through his hair.

"I like your New York accent."

"I didn't realize I still had it."

"Thanks again for taking me to the planetarium. I enjoyed the presentation," I told him.

"Actually that was my first time there. I liked it too. I like being around you," he gazed into my eyes.

"I feel the same way about you," I sparkled.

"You're different from other women I've dated. There's something about you."

"What you see is what you get. I'm just me."

"You're not an artichoke type of woman. Some women have so many layers about themselves. They're hard to figure out."

"Anyone who has that many layers must be hiding something. Which fruit do I remind you of?"

"Definitely a peach. You have a beautiful redbone skin tone on the outside and you're sweet on the inside."

"That's about right," I nodded.

"Which fruit do I remind you of?" he asked.

"My favorite fruit. As long as you're engaged to another woman you are like forbidden fruit," I smirked.

He laughed.

"What's your favorite color?" I asked.

"I like earthy shades. You know colors that resemble the outdoors, browns, rusty orange and sage. What's your favorite color?"

"My favorite color is red. I've been sort of shy in the past."

"No," he teasingly gasped.

I giggled. "I used to wear navy-blue most of the time, to blend in. Now I'm wearing brighter shades to let the world know I'm here," I motioned with my hands for emphasis.

"So red is your new favorite color," he nodded with assessing eyes.

"Yes."

"Tell me something you do well."

"I can sing and I cook well," I answered with a bright smile.

"I'd love a good home cooked meal," he hinted.

"Well, meet me at my place, Thursday evening at 6:00 p.m.," I invited.

"You're on," he smiled.

When I returned back from lunch, I was surprised to find silver, gold and red heart shaped balloons neatly tied to a basket of passion fruits that was placed on my office desk. The headline on the balloons read, "Be Mine."

All I could do was smile. I looked at the little card that came with the basket. It read, "Keeping company with you has been sweeter than the sweetest fruit. Love and peaches Curtis."

When I came home from work, I placed a Curtis Cooper CD in my stereo and turned up the volume. I admired his R&B soulful voice. Closing my eyes, I focused on my favorite song by him, "I Love Lovin' You." Then I reminisced about the first gentle kiss he gave me. I also thought about the times Curtis and I shared and my soul gave a smile.

I walked outside and sat down on my back steps, my chin in my hand, with my elbow propped on my crossed legs, thinking . . . . "Of course I love him," I told myself.

*   *   *

After Curtis and I ate the home cooked meal I promised him, we relaxed on my leather couch and made conversation.

"I loved the parmesan chicken," Curtis told me.

"Thanks. I wanted to tell you how much I loved the balloons and the passion fruit basket that you sent to my office the other day. That was the highlight of my day."

"You're the highlight of my day," he told me.

"I know you're not heterophobic. You're not secretly bi-curious or anything?" I randomly asked.

"Personally, I don't see what some men see in other men. I'm into women only. I adore the essence of a woman. For instance, I like your looks, your scent, your soft voice, your gentle touch, and your caring eyes. I find you very desirable. Need I say more?" Curtis pulled me close in a warm embrace and kissed me passionately.

The pleasure was intense. Being swept off my feet by emotions, I responded in the heat of passion and kissed him erotically. My feelings for him were so strong. I wanted him to hold me tighter, but I pulled back before we went all the way.

"No, don't spoil this perfect evening. Everything seemed so right. I feel like hopping on you like a bullfrog. Why did you start being reluctant? Did I do something that turned you off? What's wrong?" he asked.

"Oh you pushed all the right buttons." Leaning over I kissed him on the mouth. Resting my hand on his cheek, I told him, "I want you."

"I'm getting mixed signals. I don't understand why you're not bouncing on my balls right now. Are you ready for a nightcap or what? I know you said you used to be shy, but damn."

"Curtis I really, really, like you. You just don't know," I shook my head.

He started laughing.

"I'm trying to save myself for the man who truly loves me," I finely answered his question. "I want to know that the man I give the most intimate part of myself to is interested in more than just my body."

"Why?" He looked very disappointed.

"I want true love."

"You're one of those sexy-nerds. OMG! I've got one," he laughed.

"Where did you get that lingo from? Sexy-nerd," I parroted.

"That's been out there. That's older than cool-beans."

"I've heard it before. I just wondered where it came from."

"I'd like to get to know you better and see how it turns out. It takes a lot of strength to abstain from sex. I don't know how you do it," he shook his head.

"One day at a time."

There's nothing like the attraction between a man and a woman; it's something powerful.

Sometimes a man needs to be paced. I think Curtis found it surprising that I had the confidence to pace the relationship, when I thought he was going too fast. He needs to prove himself to me. I'll just bet he wants me to prove I love him too.

I affirm that I see and command the way to be cleared. May perfect love and supportiveness with lasting success now manifest in my relationship with Curtis. I now replace the partitions with true love; for I love and I am loved.

*   *   *

The potluck party my team and I had at work was a hit. It was a relaxing, fun, informal get-together that we had during our lunchtime. It doesn't necessarily have to be a special occasion for us to have a potluck; we have them just because.

Everyone who participated brought a prepared dish of food to share. I brought buttermilk bread rolls and Tuscan meatballs, which turned out to be a favorite among my group of associates.

We had a variety of dishes. Most of the food was stored at an empty cubicle close by; the rest was refrigerated. Everyone took a small portion of each food, so there would be enough for the whole group.

Mona's red-velvet cake was so delicious, yum . . . I had to cut an extra slice to take home with me. I also liked the orange salad a lot.

The potluck that we had prior, didn't go so well, because most of our group brought desert type dishes. This time around, I made a list of all the dishes each person promised to bring for the potluck, which made our get-together an overall success.

"Hello handsome," I greeted.

"May I ask who's calling?" Curtis replied.

"Your favorite flute student. You better not say the wrong name."

He laughed. "Who is this?"

"This is Joi. How was your day?"

"My day was fine. How was yours?"

"We had a potluck at work today; the food was finger licking good."

"You should have invited me."

"It was for employees of Health Gist National only."

"That's not fair," he quipped. "So what's up?"

"It was something on my mind. I never told you my age. I figure if you're interested in possibly having a romantic relationship with me, I should be honest with you. Most people assume that I'm around a decade younger than I am, because of my youthful appearance."

"I thought you looked around my age. Are you thirty-seven or thirty-eight?"

"I'm thirty-eight," I confessed.

Curtis became so quiet. There was a long silence on the other end of the phone call.

"I'm no cougar. I'm just looking for real love. I don't know any other way to be, than honest. That's the way I am."

"I admire your honesty," he finally said. "How old did you look when you were twenty?"

"I actually looked around thirteen. Adolescents used to make passes at me all the time. Cashiers always asked to see my ID at stores. It was a hoot."

"Age difference is an adolescent worry. We'd be better off forgetting about our ages and concentrating on whether the relationship works for the both of us, or not. If other people have a problem with it, let it be their problem," he told me.

"You are of age."

"Yes. I'm the man."

"You're the man."

"Your voice sounds young too. I'm shocked about our age difference, but I'll get over it," he added.

"I don't feel old. Maybe age is a state of mind in a way."

"No one would guess you're older than I am, by looking at you. You called Crystal Ma'am. Girl, you're a trip. She's still fussing about that."

"She was being annoying. So, I gave her an elbow to the rib, in so many words."

"I'm still deciding about us, okay."

"Fine. Do you ever attend church?" I asked.

"I used to, when I was young boy. My Mom used to drag me to church every Sunday morning. She taught Sunday school, so I knew just about every Bible story there was," he sighed.

"What's your favorite Bible story, that you can remember?"

"Um, the story of Esther," he replied.

"My favorite is the story of Joseph and his coat of many colors."

"I liked that one too. Now that I look back on it, Sunday school wasn't so bad after all."

"Would you like to come to my church? I mean, just one time. If you don't like it, I'll never ask you to come again. Fair enough?" I invited.

"Deal."

An usher handed a program to Curtis and I as we entered the double doors of True Righteousness Church of God.

"Hi Joi!" Tiffany waved when she caught a glimpse of Curtis and I stepping through the church congregation, trying to find a seat.

"Oh hi Tiffany," I waved back as we made our way to an open space on the eighth row.

Tiffany grew wide-eyed and sat down on a pew across the way.

We settled back and listened to the choir as they sang.

Curtis hummed along.

I liked sitting close to Curtis. I enjoyed the sweet soulful sound of his voice. His voice sure had matured since his teen-superstar years, I thought.

"That was a beautiful selection we heard from our choir. I'm going to let my light shine today," Pastor Wright opened.

"Hallelujah," a church member raised a hand.

"How many of you know if you walk in the spirit you won't fulfill the lust of the flesh?" Pastor asked the congregation.

"Amen," the congregation replied.

"If I walk in the spirit, I will live in the spirit. I wouldn't covet my neighbor's wife, if I walk in the spirit. Can I get a witness here today?" his voice rang out.

"Preach it," an elderly woman with a fancy hat on shouted with a shake of her head.

"Mrs. Betsy may be looking real good to my flesh, but I need to remind myself that she is not mine, she belongs to another," he continued on in a singsong voice and bit down on the forefinger of his clasped fist.

A little girl in the next pew covered her mouth with her hand and giggled.

"I have to tell myself if I walk in the spirit, I won't fulfill the lustful desires of the flesh. I will be faithful to my devoted wife of fourteen years," he looked over at his wife.

"Help him Lord. Help him Lord," his wife waved her hand in the air.

"Amen," I smiled.

"If I walk in the light there will be no darkness in me. In order to not fall into temptation, I remove my eyes off another man's woman and focus my eyes on my own wife."

"Amen," Curtis nodded.

"The serpent tempted Adam and Eve to bite into forbidden fruit. See, when Eve saw that the fruit was pleasant to the eyes and a tree to be desired to make her wise, her curiosity got the better of her. She took the fruit and ate it and Adam ate it too, like some idiot or something. And it cost them their lives in the Garden of Eden. They lost paradise. Curiosity got the better of Eve. Let me say, it was curiosity that killed the cat. Sometimes when temptation comes around knocking on your door, your very life could be at stake. We must beware of evil influences!"

"Yes!" a young man shouted.

"I'm saying Lord, give us this day our daily bread, lest we be tempted to bite into forbidden fruit. Amen," Pastor Wright concluded his message.

"He's a good preacher," Curtis whispered in my ear.

Pastor sure spoke a word in season that Sunday.

While I was bagging some parsley, I spotted Gege prancing down the grocery aisle. "How have you been?" I greeted.

"Girl, I'm blessed and highly favored. And you?"

"I suppose I'm blessed too," I replied.

"I have a clean bill of health today. Whatever Brent gave me was curable. I'm thankful for that. I can't complain."

"I'm still shocked about Brent."

"I am too, you think you know a person."

I nodded.

"Was that Curtis Cooper I saw you with at church last Sunday?" Gege asked.

"Yes. It was he."

"Isn't he engaged? You two looked like a couple to me. I'm just saying," she smirked.

I smiled.

"Is it, or is it not a love thing going on between you and him?"

"We're friends."

"Oh, and that's all there is to it?" she pried.

"Girl you're digging for something aren't you?" I asked.

"I saw something between the two of you."

"He told me he'd give up his fiancé for me, but that remains to be seen. Her name is Crystal, that heifer beat me to him," I sighed.

"How can you be so calm about it girl? He is so fine. That bad boy can sing," she gave me a high-five. "I used to go to his concerts all the time."

"I've been to a couple of 'em."

"I know that stank ass bitch Crystal. I've seen the two of them at clubs up in Beverly Hills. She's always droppin' names and shit. Every time I see her, she's walking with her nose up in the air. I can't stand her ass."

"She's not my favorite person either. Little Miss Sunshine herself," I said in a sarcastic tone of voice.

"She thinks she's more than she is. I hope you take him from her. I don't see why he's with that bird-faced thing."

"Tell me about it," I agreed.

"You've got good looks. Keep on working it girl."

"Maybe I could take him, if I tried hard enough," I told her.

"See, that's what I'm talking about," she laughed.

"If it happens, it happens. If it doesn't happen, I'm not gonna sweat it," I stated with a careless tone of voice. "So how's your love life?"

"Although I've learned how to search for the true qualities of a man's character through trial and error, I still have a nagging feeling that I could make another mistake. I want to be sure, you know," she sighed.

"Yeah. I could imagine."

"In the meanwhile you keep going out with Curtis."

"Yeah," I smiled.

"If you don't take him, I will," Gege said in an as a matter of fact tone of voice.

"I have to step up my game a bit."

If I have my way, I won't be playing second fiddle to Crystal for long. I know Curtis is pining to get a taste of me. Like fine wine, I get better with time. I'm going to see how this whole thing plays out.

Chapter 13

While I was locking my front door, about to head out for work, I noticed Randy sitting on my porch swing, rocking back in forth.

"I was waiting for you," he said.

"What for?"

"Why don't you take a day off from work and play hooky with me," Randy suggested.

"I'm a supervisor. I can't pull that," I told him in a stern tone of voice.

"Well, call in sick, and we'll spend the day in your house," he told me.

"I'm not sick," I narrowed my eyes at him.

"You're so damn cute," he sighed. "Are you mad at me?"

"No. Why?"

"I've been feeling a disconnect. I want you to know, I'd rather be with you than anyone else."

"How sweet," I smiled.

"I don't mean to be sweet. I'm telling you how I feel. We need to talk about these things. I'm frustrated. You're holding out on me and I don't know what to do," he choked up in tears. "I couldn't sleep cause I was thinking of you."

I walked over to him and sat down next to him. "I don't know what to tell you. You shouldn't take it personal. All I want to do is test the water before I jump in," I looked down at my wristwatch. "Look, I have to leave now or else I'll be late for work."

He grabbed my arm. "Don't forget me," he said. It seemed so eerie.

Hours later when I returned home from work, I was surprised to see Randy still sitting on my porch swing.

"Don't tell me you've been sitting out here all day," I approached him.

"No, I haven't. I left for a while and came back. Cook me another meal," he smirked.

"Only if you'll behave like a perfect gentleman," I told him.

"Alright, I won't touch your vagina. This is gonna be hard," he sighed deeply.

That evening Randy and I ate and chatted. We even played a game of scrabble. Things got a little hot and heavy. Randy lost his head, and then he found it again.

I've imagined the sexual pleasure that Curtis and Randy could bring. A lot of nights I lay awake in bed for hours from the fiery passion stirring inside me. I haven't been feeling as self-disciplined lately. I struggle about whether I should compromise my views or not. I have needs just like the next person.

I don't want to give in to a man just because I was feeling horny or I was having a weak moment. I'd regret it.

My ideal reasons for making love would be that I've found my soul mate, the man who loves me for me. He would be someone that I've come to love and sincerely know. We'd have a long-term commitment of course.

The first time I went on a date with Randy replayed in my mind days after. I was being romanced and I loved it. I felt beautiful and desired. I loved the attention that he showed me. We all love to be treated like someone special. Maybe the romance only happened in my head. Now I think all he wanted was a quickie. Curtis on the other hand might be a different story.

Thoughts of Curtis and Randy flood my mind on a day-to-day basis. I never thought I could feel this way about two men at the same time. I don't want to lose either one of them right now. A person can be momentarily seduced by an idea of something they think is wrong.

Could it be I'm falling in love with both of them? Even the thought of it seems wicked to me. Love can bring out the worse and the best in someone. It's all in my hands. Maybe I think too much.

"Why didn't you tell me you've been going out with Curtis Cooper?" Destiny asked.

"You saw us at church together right?"

"No. I didn't come to church last Sunday. Someone told me that she saw you with him."

"Destiny calm down. He's only human," I told her.

"Curtis is the finest white man I've ever seen. I'm all for racial harmony. Ooh, I love his music," she enthusiastically voiced.

I nodded.

"When you told me you were trying to hook up with someone, I never dreamed you'd snag a celebrity. What a way to find love. I'm so excited for you. How are things between you and him?"

"Things are fine."

"You like him?"

"What is there not to like about him? I mean, come on he's hot," I bragged on him.

"I know you're into him. Look at you, shining bright like a Christmas tree."

"So how's your love life?" I asked.

"Donald and I are doing fine. I'm happy and I want you to be happy too," she gave me a hug. "What's for dinner?" she asked heading for the kitchen.

"Here we go again, always inviting yourself over for dinner unexpectedly."

She laughed.

Destiny and I went on like that all the time, and it never meant anything negative. We were just comfortable enough with each other to say how we really felt about everything.

"Joi, whoever you waved at, at church made an unscheduled appearance. I think her name was Stephany or Tiffany," Curtis told me.

"Her name is Tiffany. What about her?"

"She showed up here at my place of business, wearing a pair of daisy dukes and a mid-drift. She said that I would be better served with my own kind."

"What?" I gasped. I couldn't believe what I was hearing.

"Your friend told me that I should be her man. And that whites should stick together."

"Tiffany is the kind of white girl who can't get enough of black dick. Ever since I've known her, all I've ever seen her with are black men," I told Curtis.

"She told me that we belonged together."

"Are you kidding me?" I shook my head in disbelief.

"No shit. I kid you not," he told me.

"That hypocritical, two-faced whore," I fumed with clinched fists.

"I told her that I liked my coffee with no cream. I wasn't about to take up with some hoochie white girl."

"Tiffany was supposed to have been my best friend. I feel so betrayed."

"You had a blond super-freak like her for a best friend? You know you ought to choose your friends more carefully," he placed his arms around me.

I began to bawl. I don't know what came over me. I couldn't help it.

Curtis started crying too. I felt a bond between us.

Who is this guy, Curtis Cooper? I feel good about him. He's a good man.

Step 17: Know a good man when I see one.

During my lunchtime, I walked over to Maury's Cafe like I'd do on any other workday.

"There's my girl. Let's go over to a table and talk," Tiffany told me with a bubbly attitude.

We walked over to a table near the back window.

Taking a seat, I told her, "I heard you paid Curtis a visit."

"See, what had happen was, I wanted to see if Curtis offered piano lessons, but it turned out he doesn't," she explained.

"Tiffany, you're such a liar!" I exclaimed.

"What? That is the truth," she put on this innocent act. "I saw him playing the piano on TV before."

"The nature of your visit was totally different from what you've said. Curtis told me everything. He has no reason to lie to me. What the hell is going on with you anyway?"

"If you hadn't been so bougie about having the threesome, Max and I might still be together right now," she spouted.

"Don't blame me for your failed relationship. It takes two not three, okay."

"I would've been more comfortable experimenting with you."

"Tiffany, I don't want vagina. And I'm not your guinea pig. Max has got you all confused with his threesomes," I told her.

"I'm not confused. I was attracted to you before I met Max."

"What the . . . Don't spring this on me after what you've done. Why were you making passes at Curtis? What was up with that?"

Her eyes filled up with tears. "Why does everything come so easy to you, huh?"

"Why are you so bitter?" I asked in amazement.

"You've got your nice cozy home in a good neighborhood in Valley Village, and I ended up stuck in Panorama City. I'd even be happy to find a decent place in Van Nuys. You're the kind that sails right to the top like a gas balloon. You've left me behind. You barely start dating and you manage to snag a catch like Curtis Cooper, of all people," she bared her dirty soul.

"Uh, I thought you would be okay with it. You told me before that you didn't like white men. Why is Curtis any different? And why did you tell him that whites should stick together, when you knew I liked him?"

"A man is a man, is a man," she voiced sarcastically.

"So you want all the black men and white men too?"

"No, I don't," she replied with an attitude.

"Well, you could have fooled me. I thought we were best friends. Tiffany, you better be glad I want to be Christian-like. I could kill you for this," I whispered to her. "Hey, I'm not the one for you to mess with. Just stay out of my business, okay." I held my hands up, with a hands off attitude. Then I stood up from the table and turned my back on the friendship Tiffany and I once shared.

Step 18: Let go of jealous two-faced friends.

She lost a true friend that day. They say, "All things work out for the good." It's probably best we're not friends anymore. Tiffany had such a kind looking face, but she was a devil in disguise. Looks can be deceiving. I've learned my lesson.

It's my life, everything I want and more. To everything else I shut the door. I disconnect from all that ills. I am the deal. All the mylns stumble and fall. I shall remain standing tall. No loss that I'd miss. I give life my kiss.

Chapter 14

I'm a go-getter. If I see something I want, I'm going after it. My aggressive business nature and desire for independence has made me a financial success. My Father made me the sole proprietor of Kennedy Construction because he knew I could handle the responsibility. Business has been good. I'm able to buy all the toys I want. It's a good life.

When my Father says he's proud of me, it means the world to me. Earlier in life he has been the motivating force behind my desire to do well in life. I'm like my Father in some ways. For one, I always want things organized a certain way; if it's not the way I want it, I get mean. He's a control freak, but I don't think I am. If I can pick a good woman to be with, then he'd know that I can handle my business in every area of my life.

All this thinking reminds me of Joi. My cut-to-the-chase mentality is not helping when it comes to her. She's my newest fascination. Joi gives me the sweetest sensations. I'd never want her to know how much power she has over me. I get weak in the knees from just one look at her. Her beauty captivates me. I just know my Mom would like her. She has a good head on her shoulders.

"Inna, have you drawn up the proposal for the Nolan account yet?" I spoke to my secretary over the intercom.

"Yes I have. I'll bring a hardcopy right in," she replied in a voice so sweet.

"Good. I should have submitted it yesterday," I replied.

"I'm printing it now."

Ah, she strutted into my office looking ever so beautiful. "Thanks, Inna. You're a lifesaver," I told her.

"You're welcome," she smiled at me as she handed over the documents. "Is there anything else?"

"No. I'm all set for now." I smacked her on the ass.

She giggled. "Let me know if you need anything." Her eyes floored me. Inna twisted her hips as she pranced out my office, emulating the sensuality of a sex kitten.

Since I'm single again, I'm sure glad I have my secretary to rely on for booty calls, especially since I've been dating Miss Virginal girl. I don't get her. She has me on some type of probation. Joi has her pussy on lock down, but she said love is the key that will open it. I don't know if I love her, but I want her. I groped her good while I was over her house the other night. I pressed myself up close to her body and something inside me went off like fireworks. She really got turned on, I heard her inhale. Joi must have felt something for me too. She might give me some. I'll keep working on her.

"Call on line two," Inna voiced over the intercom.

"Kennedy Construction," I answered.

"Hello Randy. This is Mr. Powers."

"Oh yes. How are you?"

"Good. And yourself?"

"Couldn't be better," I chuckled.

"I'd like for construction to began in the fall."

"That's right around the corner. The ball is in your court, Mr. Powers."

From time to time, I schedule meetings with my financial planner. Rick's a good one. He's got my back.

"So, if there is an investment opportunity which may do well for you, wouldn't you want to take advantage of it?" Rick asked.

"Of course," I replied.

"You're a speculative type of investor, which means you're a gambler."

"Don't label me man. Look, my Dad told me that mutual funds are low risk. Hook me up with a few of those. I want my money to make money," I told him.

"Diversify. Good choice," he scribbled on his note pad. "You manage your money well."

"I don't know. I've hired you to do that for me, because you're in the financial field. Rick, you're the one with the series 65 license, not me."

"I get you," he paused. "All I care about is the bottom line, nothing more and nothing less. I'm only out for your best interest."

"Good. How are my stocks doing?" I asked.

"Your pharmaceutical stock crashed. Your IPO stock is doing well at this point. Your overall invested capital is making a good financial performance," he explained.

I exhaled and relaxed. "Well that's all I wanted to hear. My main concern is remaining liquid. Give me a print out of my investment status, will you?"

"I'm on it right now. Hey, I work for you. You're the big boss around here. Randy, I'm here to make sure you succeed."

"As long as you understand that," I grinned and shook his hand.

Now that I have so much on my plate, so much is at stake.

While I was relaxing on my living room couch, watching a classic blacksploitation film on TV, my brother Reggie dropped by with some women of the night. I had already downed a couple of beers so I was ready for anything.

"He's cute," one of the whores told my brother.

"Is it true that your new girlfriend is not putting out?" Reggie asked me.

"Yep. She told me that she wants to be in love with the man that she fucks," I answered.

"Which one of these bitches do you want? I like both of them, so it doesn't matter to me," Reggie said.

"I'll take the one wearing the purple. She has a nice ass on her," I told him.

"Woo turn around for me baby," Reggie told the one wearing the purple.

She did a 360-degree turn around.

"Hot damn. She does have a tight ass. I'll do her after you," Reggie said.

"Reggie, I'll kill you if Joi finds out I'm a womanizer. Don't tell the guys about this. I know she wouldn't want me if she knew. I'm scared she'll find out," I told him.

"If she wants an exclusive love, than why bother. Just because Gwen broke your heart, why break this new chick's heart? From what I've heard she seems nice," he said.

"I don't know what I want to do. I think I might love her a little. I'm serious about her."

"My lips are sealed. Blood is thicker than water," he told me.

"Come here you pretty nasty girl. Let's play house," I told her.

She giggled and brought her stank ass over to me. I got a good fuck out of her.

Later on, Reggie told me that the one he had smelt like shit and that the fuck sucked.

I think most of those kind of bitches don't like men anyway. All they want is a quick buck.

It's so hard to find a good woman these days. I want a little something more than sex too. I think I might be willing to change for Joi.

Friday evening, I decided to go out bowling with the fellows. The moment I walked inside the bowling alley, I spotted an interracial couple. They were hugged up, laughing and chatting. From a distance the woman looked like Joi. So I walked over to them for a closer look. Damn, it was Joi with another man.

To save face, I walked over and said hello to her, just to let her know she was busted.

I can't explain exactly how it felt to see her in the arms of another man, but it was like all the wind had been knocked out of me. That was a low blow to my image.

I got a good look at the guy she was with. He used to sing years ago. His name was Curtis Cooper. I could have spit nails.

Chapter 15

Curtis told me that he was going to Funville Bowling Alley to tighten up his game. He invited me to tag along. Since I had never gone bowling before, I decided I'd go just to try something new.

"See Joi, you place your fingers in the bowling ball holes like this. Walk quickly up to this line here, and then throw the ball. Your aim is to knock down as many pens as you can in one throw," Curtis explained.

"I can do that," I smiled. Picking up one of the bowling balls, I did exactly what he told me and I hit four pens. "Whoa!" I screamed.

"Not bad for a first try," he clapped. "Okay, now watch me," he jumped up from his seat, took a ball and threw it quickly down the lane. "Yes! I made a strike!" He jumped up and down.

"You are good. I'd love to do that," I told him.

"Since you liked the display of my bowling skills so much, I'm going to do more." Curtis rolled the bowling ball down the lane again. "Strike!" He raised a fist in the air and brought it down in an I won motion.

"You knocked down all the pens again!" I shouted. "Bowling is fun. I like it."

"I thought you looked like a fun loving woman," he looked at me with eyes so blue.

"I do?" I raised my eyebrows.

"Yes," he nodded. "You always look like you're about to laugh. Crystal would never go out bowling with me. And she always scowls like this," Curtis made a frown.

I laughed. "I wonder why she doesn't like bowling."

He shrugged his shoulders. Then he broke out into a serenade, "Chances are, cause I wear a funny grin, the moment you come into view." He laughed.

I clapped for him. I never realized he had such a funny sense of humor. It was nice finding out what Curtis's personality was like.

Step 19: Don't be a killjoy like Crystal.

"Let's sit down and talk a bit." He placed his arm around my shoulders. "You're so beautiful," he kissed me on the lips with gentle passion.

My heart leaped with pleasure. I felt myself getting lost in his kiss.

We walked over and took a seat.

"I had no idea that a woman like you still existed," he said, cuddling me in his arm.

"What kind of woman is that?"

"A virtuous woman," he replied.

"Thank you for the compliment," I smiled.

"Your smile is like a ray of sunshine. Keep on shining girl."

"I like your smile too." Glancing around, I noticed Randy was there watching us like a hawk.

"OMG!" I gasped to myself.

"OMG, what?" Curtis asked.

It felt like time stood still for a few seconds. Randy walked directly over to us and said, "Hello," with an angry expression on his face.

"Hi Randy," I whimpered.

He did an about-face turn around and marched right out the bowling alley exit.

"Ah oh. You're in trouble," Curtis smirked.

"Oh damn," I raised my right hand to my mouth. "He wasn't a happy camper that's for sure," I remarked out of nervousness.

"He looked at me with eyes like daggers. Have you dated him before?" Curtis asked with extreme interest.

"Yes," I nodded.

"Is he the guy you wrote the poem about?"

"Which?" I questioned, feeling puzzled.

"The one about special moments."

"Curtis has anyone ever told you that you have the memory of an elephant?"

"Just answer my question," he demanded.

"Yes, he is," I admitted.

"Joi, don't let him come between us. I want to keep on seeing you," he told me in a serious tone of voice.

"Of course we'll keep seeing each other. I have flute lessons with you."

"You know that's not what I mean," he stated in a slightly angry tone. "I like the person I am, whenever I'm with you; I don't feel all stressed out. I can be myself. I can relax," he added.

"I'm glad I make you feel that way."

"Has anyone ever told you that you are so calming?"

"Yes. It's because of my customer service background. I'm a Customer Service Supervisor, who's professionally trained to defuse irate members regarding escalated issues. I calm down angry customers for a living, among other things."

"I know you must be good at it," he smiled.

"As a matter of fact I am," I tooted my horn, beep. "I'm going to need those skills to deal with Randy."

"Why don't you kick Randy to the curb?"

"This is a complicated situation. I really need to think this over," I sighed.

"I know it makes me seem like a flip-flop, because I'm still with Crystal and I'm dating you. But I've struggled with this so much, because I'm not a flip-flop. There's something about you, and I can't let you slip out of my hands."

"I don't want to lose you either," I gazed into his alluring eyes. "I just spotted two of Randy's friends giving me the evil eye. I think we better leave," I told Curtis.

"Why would they be mad at you?" he asked.

"They wanted me to hook up with Randy."

Shortly after we called it a night.

There was a long silence between us during the drive to my house. I guess we both had a lot to think about.

We got out of his black Infinity and walked slowly up the sidewalk. We stopped for a moment and faced each other. Standing a stone's throw away from a street lamp, Curtis stepped closer and my heart started beating faster. He took me in his arms, and we kissed for a few minutes. Curtis tried so hard to suppress his natural urges. We finally made it to my front door.

I noticed Randy's white pickup truck parked up the street. "I think we have company. That's Randy's truck. He's most likely in there." I peered down the road at his vehicle.

"Now he has you under surveillance. I'm still feeling that look he gave me. Be careful," he kissed me on the lips.

I nodded. "You too."

"I'll be on my way."

"See you," I waved. I watched after him as he drove away. Randy's truck didn't leave. I entered my home and locked my front door.

As soon as I settled down on my couch, the phone ranged.

"Hello," I answered.

"Joi, how come you're dating both of us at the same time?" Randy asked with a crack in his voice.

"Why are you interrogating me? You might be seeing other people too."

"How do you know that?" he asked in a suspicious tone of voice.

"Are you?" I questioned.

"I thought we had something going," he avoided answering my question.

"He's my friend, alright."

"Has he gotten any yet?" he asked.

"Randy, you're so nasty."

He chuckled. "If you think he's going out with you just to be friends, you're wrong. I know he wants you, I can feel it," he raised his voice.

"Geez laweez! Randy, give me a break."

"Isn't he that singer, Curtis Cooper? I've read somewhere that he's engaged."

"Oh really," I said sarcastically.

"Tell you what, let's call Crystal up and see what she thinks about you dating her fiancé," his voice gradually became louder. The way he did the crescendo thing with his voice was unnerving.

"Randy, don't do this to me."

"Do what? My stomach is all tide up in knots about this. I want you, okay. I feel like I'm being cheated on all over again. I can't take this," he yelled at the top of his lungs.

"Lower your voice, please," I told him with a calm tone of voice. "Randy I'm sorry about what happened between you and your ex-girlfriend, but don't punish me because of her."

"Are you saying that nothing's going on between you two?"

"It's not deep right now. That's all I can say."

"What is your definition of deep?" he asked.

"We're not exclusive."

"All right. So it sounds like you have a choice to make."

"I got that."

"What are you gonna do? I wanna know where I stand," he said.

"I'll think this through."

"You come back to me, you hear," he sobbed.

"Goodnight Randy."

"Night."

My heart felt torn between Curtis and Randy. I had no idea what I was going to do. The whole situation was so unsettled. I cried myself to sleep, because I didn't want to hurt either one of them. I felt so confused.

I woke up with tears in my eyes and reached over to stop the sound of the alarm clock on my bedside table. I hesitantly threw back the covers and forced myself up. Trying to control the emotion that I felt welling up in me, tears began to flow.

Walking into the bathroom, I let out a loud cry. I couldn't keep myself from crying. Feeling a release, I splashed water on my face and dabbed my skin with a towel. Looking in the mirror with red sad eyes, I forced a smile. "Somehow I'll make the right choice. I love myself enough to not be too hasty," I told myself.

I needed to do something to get my mind off the troublesome love triangle I was in, so I decided to go to the gym. A good workout would surely relieve some of the stress I felt about the situation.

Working up a huge sweat at the gym, I felt purified. Afterwards, I went home and took a rejuvenating bubble bath.

After my bath, I used a little aromatherapy to calm the negative energies. Lavender is a fragrance that always makes me feel calm.

To feel safer, I made arrangements to have a security alarm system installed in my home.

"May we skip your flute lesson today and just talk?" Curtis asked.

"Sure."

"So what are you going to do about the stalker?" he asked.

"I assume you're talking about Randy."

"Yeah," he grumbled.

"I told him that I would think it through."

"What does that mean?"

"I'm thinking over what I should do."

"Joi don't give me up for him. I know I'm not exactly available, but I can change that," he told me.

"The way things are now, I could end up losing both of you. I need something sure."

"Oh, damn it," he fumed.

Step 20: Be smart about the situation.

As I walked out the Health Gist National corporate office transparent glass double doors, I noticed Randy sitting at one of the outdoor umbrella-tables on the grounds.

"Hey, I've been waiting here for you," he called out.

"What for?" I paused.

"To talk."

I walked up behind him and placed my arms around him over his shoulders. I rested my chin on his shoulder blade and said, "Let's talk."

"Oh, your arms feel so good around me," he caressed my arms. "Do you truly find me attractive?"

"Yes," I kissed him on the cheek.

"So, what is it then? Are you playing hard to get? Don't you want a piece of me? I mean how can you resist me?"

"Believe me, it hasn't been easy by any means. I want something more than a meaningless fling. When I do have sex I want it to mean more than animal passion."

"Bing, that's it. Animal passion is exactly the way I feel about you," he told me in a serious tone of voice. He went on, "I've been rethinking a lot of things since you've been in my life. You've helped me see that there's more to life than just a good fuck or bad fuck. I would go out bowling with you. I don't want you to see me like some sex demon. Are you following me?"

"Yes. It's about learning how to get along outside the bedroom and inside the bedroom. That's not to say that I don't have feelings for you, because I do. You have awakened feelings in me that I've never felt before. There have been nights when I couldn't fall asleep because I was thinking of you and wanting you." I caressed his cheek with the back of my thumb.

"Damn, I'm so hard right now. Do you touch yourself? You know I can do that for you. See, I could relieve your sexual tension. Do you ever have wet dreams about me?" he asked.

"Shut up. You're about to make me forget we're in a public place."

He laughed. "When I'm in my office sitting at my desk, a lot of times I'm not able to focus on my work, because I can't stop thinking of you. That's why I came over your house early in the morning the other day. I feel like I'm obsessed with you and I'm afraid of the way I feel."

"I have a lot of feelings for you too, but I don't know if we're right for each other. I'm still trying to figure out what I'm going to do," I removed my arms off of him and sat down beside him.

"I think I love you. Whatever you do, don't let me go," he gazed at me with his sexy gray eyes. Then he kissed me.

His kiss drove me crazy. I wanted to be loved and held close. Randy was starving for me and I really felt like letting him feast . . . .

Late that night my cell phone rung.

"Hello," I answered.

"It's 1:00 a.m., why do you sound wide awake? Joi you're thinking about me aren't you?" Randy asked.

"What if I am?" I whispered in a sexy tone voice.

"Ah, I knew it. I'm feeling your vibes baby."

Shyness came over me and I disconnected the call.

Men tend to want the woman who seems out of reach. I had become Randy's fantasy. I am his desire and he's my delight.

Chapter 16

My Mom once told me, "It takes more than being beautiful to get a good man, you have to be smart about it too," she tapped the side of her head with her index finger.

I don't know if Randy is the one or not. Maybe he's a diamond in the rough. Curtis could be the one if he wasn't engaged.

I remember what Gege told me about Brent, that she never felt peace about marrying him. She was lucky to have found out the secret he had been keeping before she married him.

Gut feelings should never be ignored. Whoever I choose I'm going to make sure I feel peace about it. My gut feelings have never led me wrong. If I feel uneasy, then something's sleazy. A woman's intuition is a powerful thing. Knowing power, is mine.

Step 21: Always follow my gut feelings.

* * *

Last night I came up with another step in my plan. Curtis is going to think of me as a keeper. As long as he's engaged to Crystal, I know I haven't won him over yet.

Step 22: Win over Curtis and get him to dump Crystal.

Since I'm not wowing Curtis with sex as of yet, I'll wow his stomach with good home cooked meals. If the stomach is the way to a man's heart, maybe the picnic I'm planning will do the trick. I'll delight his taste buds with a romantic meal out in the great outdoors.

Curtis and I decided to go to Balboa Park in Encino, California. Balboa Park has it all: a lake, river, picnic areas and more. I think it's the most beautiful park I've ever been too.

We made our way to the picnic area and I placed a tablecloth over one of the tables. Then I sat the basket of food on top of the table.

"I'm glad the sun finally came out," I looked up at the sky.

"As long as I'm with you it's a lovely day," Curtis smiled at me. "So what did you bring?"

"Homemade guacamole dip, chips, cheese and meat antipasto platter, ciabatta bread, chilled lemonade and chocolate covered strawberries for desert," I placed the food and the thermos cooler of lemonade on the table.

"No wine?"

"I thought lemonade would be safer, being that one of us has to drive home."

"Thoughtful, I like that. Let's eat," he cheerfully said, dipping a chip into the guacamole.

"I hope you like the guacamole."

He nodded. "It's good."

I dipped a chip in the guacamole and munched.

"Joi may I ask why you put this picnic together for me?"

"I'm a nostalgic type of person; a bit of a romantic. I like doing some things the way they used to. There was a time when couples used to go out on picnics regularly for romantic dates," I told him.

"So you see us as a couple?" he asked.

"Don't you?"

"Maybe," he looked away. "Have you dated much before?"

"Not much," I replied.

"It's strange that someone attractive as you is still unattached."

"Many hopefuls have knocked on my heart's door, but now I've decided to open up."

"Hypothetically speaking, I breakup with Crystal, and she moves out my house. Then I'd like for you to move in with me after I breakup with Crystal. What would you say to that?" Curtis asked.

"I don't believe in living together before marriage," I bluntly replied.

"Don't you test drive a car before you buy it?"

"Yes, but it's not the same."

"Well, if I breakup with Crystal would you choose me or Randy?"

"I'd choose you, because we connect in so many ways."

"I feel the same way about you," his eyes welled up with tears. "I might as well be living alone. Crystal is so unorganized; I have to handle all the bills. She wants me to hire a maid. We live in a three-bedroom house, for the sake of argument."

"I'm organized. I pay all my bills on time, and I have no problem with doing housework," I told him.

"She won't pick up a broom, but she has no problem picking up my credit card and charging it to the max."

"No worries sweetheart. It's not even that deep," I assured him.

Step 23: Don't be a deadbeat like Crystal.

"I need someone like you in my life. What about us having sex?"

"It'll happen when I think it's the right time for us."

"I know you're gonna make me wait."

"I think I'm worth the wait. A strong relationship consist of love, social interests, trust and respect, not just sex. I'd love you as much outside the bedroom as in it," I told him.

"I'm willing to wait until you're ready," he sighed.

"I'll make it worth the wait," I flirted with my eyes.

"Thanks for the incentive," he smiled. "Did I hear you say love?" he asked.

"Yes. I love you," I smiled.

"It sounded like you meant that," his face lit up.

"With all of my heart," I gazed into his blue eyes.

"Does that mean that you've oust Randy?"

"Let's just say, when you breakup with Crystal, Randy and I won't be going out again."

"Fair enough," he smiled.

"I think so," I nodded.

"I love you too," he mumbled.

"What? Did you say love?" I quipped.

"I love you!" he shouted. "With you, love isn't just a word in a song."

I stood up and made my way around the picnic table to Curtis and kissed him. Curtis kissed me back in a way that I'd never known before. My whole body perspired. He touched me in places that I'd never allowed any man to touch before. "Curtis we're giving the passersby a live peepshow," I mumbled.

He laughed.

We sat back down at the table. My body was still singing from his passionate kiss and sensual touch.

"We did get a little carried away. It's just that you're so sweet," he told me.

I began to cry.

"What's wrong?"

"Today, I'm happy, more than I've been for ages," I told him.

"Ah," he cooed.

Who knew I'd find love through new interests? Love belongs to me. I've learned there are so many ways I can grow as a person and have love in my life too.

Curtis and Randy have most likely been with a number of women. The way things are nowadays, telling either one of them that I'm a virgin could make him think that I'm not experienced enough to please him in the bedroom. I know what I'm capable of, and my aim would be to please.

Understanding sex comes natural to me. I'm in touch with all the emotions of it. I suppose it's a built in instinct. I've had a lot of orgasms since I've been wanting them. I'm sure I could satisfy their deepest longings. I've got a book about sexual positions; I think that's all I'd need. I know my sexual satisfaction would be guaranteed with either one of them. I'm filled with great anticipation.

Love is more than emotion. Love is an attribute of the daring heart. I'd hate to give all my love and pure sensual passion to an unworthy subject.

"I heard that you and Michelle got into it at the club the other night."

"A friend of mine told me she was after Donald, so I confronted her about that shit at the club, and then it was on. I kicked that bitch's ass." Destiny's expression clouded with anger.

"So that's what all the drama was about. Destiny, don't you know you could have got put in jail for that?" I warned.

"She hit me too. We both could have gotten locked up. I lost control for a moment. I was so mad at her, I saw red," she fumed.

"I know how it is when a man is involved. Situations like that could cause you to do things you otherwise wouldn't do. When I heard what happened I said that doesn't sound like the Destiny I know."

She raised a hand to her forehead. "Uh, I feel so negative right now."

"What did Donald say about all this?"

"He told me he wouldn't cheat on me. I can actually trust him," her eyes welled up with tears.

"That kind of love is rare nowadays," I told her.

"Ain't it though? He's my true love. There's no one else for me but him."

"I know I'll have my confrontations too, being with a man like Curtis."

"I wouldn't let him out of my sight if I were you. I never talk about negative things in my home. Go get some of your lavender oil to calm the negative energy in this room."

"Sure." Before leaving the room to get the fragrance I paused to say, "Destiny, you're going through a bit of a funk right now, but this too will pass," I mimicked the positive attitude she usually had.

"Shut up," she laughed.

"Here's the scented oil," I returned to the living room. "You know I was thinking about us having a me-day together at a relaxing place," I suggested.

"Yeah. We could hang out at a cafe or a quiet bookstore with a lounge area."

I nodded. "Maybe we could get our hair done."

"That sounds like fun," Destiny smiled.

In the middle of the madness, she managed to hold on to her true love. I'm happy for her. I think she has a good thing going with Donald.

Running to answer my doorbell, I was shocked when I saw Tiffany at the door.

"I want to start by saying I'm sorry. And that you're the best friend I've ever had. What I've done is unforgivable and I'll never forgive myself for being so mean to you," Tiffany blurted out.

"A friend doesn't make passes at another friend's man. It's some kind of unwritten code of friendship," I told her.

"I know I was wrong. Don't hate me forever," she pouted.

"It's apparent that we can't be friends anymore. I opened up my life to you and you tried to ruin it."

"Didn't I say I was sorry?"

"You are sorry, a sorry excuse for a friend."

"I didn't even have sex with him, and you're going to end our friendship like that?"

"What friendship?" I asked. "It's the principle of the matter. You tried Curtis, but for some reason he didn't fuck you. Anything could have happened."

"What makes you so sure nothing happened?" She looked at me as if she wanted me to doubt him.

"A dog wouldn't have told me anything about you coming by, that's for sure," I replied with an as a matter of fact tone of voice. "Not not be not. Not you, not you. You are not the one. No no no, you go. Get out of my life."

"Why don't you let me in smart ass? I need to learn some shit from you," she smirked.

"Tiffany, I don't wish to be acquainted with you anymore."

"Joi, sometimes the heart craves both good and evil. I love you," she cried.

"I could never trust you again," I became teary eyed. "Bye Tiffany," I calmly told her and closed my front door.

I sat down on my couch by the end-table lamp with my journal in hand and began to pray.

Dear God,

Oh giver of love, hear me as I pray tonight. Please make everything turn out right. The hearts of two men I have won, help me choose the right one. I never thought I'd come between Curtis and the drama queen. Lord you know that woman is mean. I'm better for him or so it seems. Randy, oh he looks like a dream. Could he be my prince, my king? Curtis he is so fine too. I'd love for him to be my Boo. Oh God, what should I do? Please give me a sign, some kind of clue. Whores, you can't take my man. Leave him alone. He's mine, you understand. Almighty One, let the mystery be revealed, let my love be fulfilled. Bend the right one's path to me, from all roadblocks set him free. Be the restorer of his soul. Let our love be fine like gold. Amen.

Chapter 17

I went to a local bar to try and clear my head. Crystal was like an old bathrobe that I had become used to, a love-hate relationship. It seems kind of funny, that if I had never met Joi I would have settled for a dull mundane marriage with Crystal.

Joi's desire to find emotional, intellectual and sexual compatibility fascinates me. Her self-imposed religious convictions and philosophical leanings even turn me on.

Stepping up to the counter, I settled on a high round bar stool.

"What will you have today?" the bartender asked.

"I'll have a martini on the rocks," I ordered.

"What's up Curtis?" Chuck, an old friend of mine from the music industry took a seat on the next bar stool to the right and ordered a drink.

"The same ol' same ol'. How have you been Chuck?"

"Things aren't going so well right now, but I'm lookin' up. Just the other day I was wondering what ever happened to you," he said.

"Life is happening to me," I told him.

"I'm almost sure Intergalactic Sound Records would want to work out a new recording contract with you. A lot of the singers out right now sound manufactured. You were a natural. You had your own style and you did it well," he told me.

"Thanks for the vote of confidence."

"You either got it or you don't. Curtis you've got what it takes," he nodded and sipped his drink. "Fan mail still comes in for you. The ladies are crazy about you. Tell you what, here's my business card if you want to discuss this further."

"I'm open to considering it," I nodded.

"This is going to create quite a buzz," he said.

"I'd sure look forward to working with you again, if I do make a come back. You always found or produced great material for me," I gave an optimistic smile.

"We'll talk," Chuck sipped his drink.

"There's nothing like an early morning jog," I said as I tried to keep a study pace.

"I'd rather be asleep in bed," Crystal muttered.

"Stormy, let the sun come out," I sighed.

"Fuck you," she snapped.

"Why do you always have to make a chore out of every activity we share?"

"That's not true," she rolled her eyes at me.

"Believe it or not this is something I need to do. I'd like to have your cooperation for a change."

"You don't have to run like this," she scoffed.

"Working out like this will give me the stamina I need to sing and dance on stage with no sweat. So contrary to what you've said, I do need to run like this. Do I have your support or what?" I asked.

"Whatever. Hold up for a minute. Let me take a sip of water," she paused to drink some bottled water.

"Running like this is kind of tough. I'll take it easy on you," I paused to take a sip of water. "We can head back."

"Finally," she let out a flustered breath.

"Curtis, sing the last verse once again," Harold, the producer said as he mixed the recording.

"Okay." I sung the verse.

"Curtis has perfect pitch," Chuck bragged on me as he watched through the recording studio window.

"Are you pleased with all the mixes I've done?" I asked.

"It's damn good," Chuck laughed.

Ever since I was a young teen growing up in New York City, I've wanted to be in some facet of the music industry. My love for music developed at an early age. As a youngster my Mom always had some type of music playing in the house, from gospel to R&B. That's how I learned how to sing like black people. In my teen singing sensation years they called me Blue-Eyed Soul.

I'm ashamed to admit it, but there was a period in my life when I dealt drugs. My boys called me soft when I decided to get out of the business. Luckily, I changed direction in time. Shortly after, my running buddies, Rico and Bug-eye, got sent to prison on possession of drug charges. My Mom used to call me a God-blessed child.

It's strange that when you're walking down the road of life and you take a little turn to the left and you see what that path has to offer you. Then you realize that you've made a wrong turn. Sometimes it's so hard to make it back to the right road. It's a sad thing that some never make it back to the main road again.

Music is like my salvation. It has kept me out of trouble. Music is my best friend. I was so happy when my parents arranged for me to go to a school of performing arts. My Dad used to say, "An idle mind is the devil's workshop."

My Dream

It was birthed inside
my soul.
No one could take
my dream.
My dream held on
through the highs
and lows.
No one could take
my dream.
The door opened for me.
Oh yeah.
My dream has
become reality.
My dream was
meant to be.
No one could take
my dream.

* * *

"Let's take the dance routine from the top," the choreographer directed.

I nodded and followed Janell's lead as she ran through the dance routine.

"That was smooth!" I shouted.

"You're in good shape," she told me.

"I work out. It ain't no thing."

"You're ready to get back on stage huh?"

"Girl, I was born ready."

"Let's call it a day. I have to pick up my daughter from daycare," she said.

"I'm good. I've got the routine down," I told her.

"Have a good one." She grabbed her gym bag and was out the door.

"You too."

Purpose

Like an eagle, I
stand on a
high rock, ready
to soar into
my place in life.
The wind beneath
my wings
is guiding me
right into
my purpose.

"Welcome back to Intergalactic Sound Records. Dinner's on me," Chuck said.

"It's good to be back," I told him.

"So do you have a woman in your life?" he asked.

"Actually there's two women in my life."

"Play on, player," he laughed.

"It's not like that. I'm about to breakup with one of them," I told him.

"Why?"

"My new lady friend told me that she'd stop seeing the guy she's been seeing and get with me if I breakup with my fiancé."

"So you're playing let's make a deal and shit. Your new lady friend must be hot," he said.

"She's better than the bitch I'm about to breakup with."

"I'm engaged myself. She does it for me. I'm happy with her."

A tall redhead approached our table. "Hi you two. I thought you looked familiar. Do I know you from some place?" she asked me.

"No. I don't know you," I glanced at her.

"Do you wanna know me?" She winked an eye at me.

"No. I'm not interested," I shook my head.

"Oh well, it's your loss," she snapped. "Say, you're kind of cute. What's your name?" she asked Chuck.

"Chucky baby," he answered.

"How about a nightcap?" she asked him.

"No thanks."

"You two must be gay or something," she said.

"No, we have good taste," I told her.

She walked away.

Chuck laughed. "That was a good one."

"Chuck, I hate when stank whores like her try to accuse me of being gay just because I don't want their dirty asses. That pisses me off."

"It's a tactic their desperate asses use to get some. It's like a dare or something," Chuck said.

"It's a mind game. Apparently no one is knocking down her door to get her worn out pussy," I told him.

"Apparently not. I wouldn't risk losing my sweet Pelar for a tramp like her, anyway. I'd probably end up with a sick dick messing around with that twitch."

"I was thinking of you the other night and I couldn't seem to fall asleep. It was just one of those things. Anyway, all of a sudden I felt inspired to write a song," I told her.

"Now I'm your inspiration?" Joi asked.

"Joi, don't you know you're the rift to my rhythm, the song in my heart."

She blushed. "Curtis you're the cream in my coffee. You're my white chocolate."

"Oou. Want to taste some?"

She kissed me and set all my senses on fire. Joi sparks the greatest feelings in me. "The new song I composed is called "I Want You." It took around a hour to write."

"I want you too," she gave me a sexy smile. "May I hear the song please?"

I sung the song directly to her.

I Want You

When I am with you,
I can be myself.
Don't want to be someone else, mh.
You're sweet like ginger and spice.
I want you in my life.

I love you. Mmh mmh mh mh mh mh.
I want you. Mmh mmh mh mh.
You make me want to be true.
Oh baby, give it all to you.

"That's just a taste of it," I smiled into her coffee brown eyes.

"All I can say is wow. You're better than good. I loved it." She placed her head on my shoulder.

"Thank you." I put my arm around her firm waistline.

"Thank you for the song," she looked into my eyes.

As we sat on the hood of my car, for a mesmerizing moment it seemed as if time stood still.

"So, where were you yesterday evening? I was waiting here for you. You didn't leave a note or anything," Crystal gave me the third degree.

"You started an argument with me earlier that day, so I left and drove around."

"Are you telling me that you drove around all evening?" She eyed me suspiciously. "I know that's some bullshit."

"Look Crystal, I can't take it anymore. This constant nagging is driving me up the wall. I can't find peace in my own home."

"Darling, I'm not nagging you. I simply asked you a question," she said in her own snooty way.

"Crystal, I'm unhappy. This whole thing is not working out," I told her.

"It's not working out? Well, three months ago you said that we were a perfect fit."

"If I said that, I was temporarily insane. Look, we've been together for two years. We do the same thing day in and day out. Whenever I make a suggestion to spice up things a little, you never implement it. Hey, if you don't care, I don't care," I raised my hands in the air.

"But Curtis I do care."

"I know that this is as good as it's ever going to get between us. If you think any different, you're only fooling yourself," I looked her straight in the eyes.

"It's another woman. I know it," she raised an accusing index finger my way.

"Baby, this is about you. It's about the way you disrespect me. You're never supportive of me. I deserve better."

"I do respect you."

"Well, if you respect me, why do you keep doing things that irk me every time I turn around? You don't respect my place of business. You disrespect my clients. Remember the time when you harassed my student named Joi simply for being early. She wasn't rushing me. She was patiently waiting for her flute lesson. I don't even want to think about the way you abruptly come in nearly every time I give Megan her voice lesson. It's so embarrassing. Your shit stinks too," I exasperated. I was fed up.

"So what are you saying Curtis?"

"I'm saying that I'm calling off our engagement. I don't love you anymore. I've had enough of you. Crystal, it's better that we've realized we're not good for each other now, than later. Pack up your stuff and get out my house!" I ordered.

"No. We're going to get married and have a family," she cried. She stood up from the bed and jumped on my back.

I slung her off my back. It was almost like watching a movie. "Give me my keys," I grabbed the keys off the dresser. "Give me back that engagement ring." I forced the ring off her finger. "I'll help you pack your things."

"No, don't do this!" she screamed. She bawled like a spoiled kid that didn't get her way. "Where will I go?" she blew her nose.

"Go stay with one of your friends, for all I care. You're not staying here."

"So what are you going to do about that?" she pointed at my erected penis.

I quickly grabbed a magazine off the bedside table to cover up.

"I know you haven't been fucking whoever she is. She's been blue-balling you," she cackled like a hen. Then Crystal peered at me with her light brown catty eyes.

Damn, I was tempted to fuck her one last time, but she could have gotten pregnant.

"I've called off my engagement with Crystal," I told my Dad.

"All I can say is follow your heart."

"I've been seeing another woman. Her name is Joi. She's there for me emotionally. We understand each other."

"If you've found a woman that you can understand, you're doing well. I'm still trying to understand your Mom."

"Mom didn't like Crystal anyway."

"Don't rush into anything."

"Believe me, we're taking it slow," I told him.

"I hope you've picked a white girl this time. You know I don't support interracial marriage," Mom walked into the living room.

"Lighten up honey. We're all of the human race," Dad said.

"Joi is a beautiful woman of color. She's a nice virtuous woman. Give her a chance Mom," I told her.

"Why don't you like white women? Is it something I've done?" she asked.

"No Mom. Don't take it personal. I just simply prefer women of color."

"You always were a nigger lover," she cried.

"Mom, it's only color. You're no better than anyone else. Why did you listen to black gospel music while I was growing up, if you're so against them?"

"For entertainment. They're good entertainers," she scoffed.

"Some Christian you are. Dad I've got to go. Mom always does this to me. Bye." I stood up from the armchair.

"If she's all you said she is, I want to meet her," she told me.

"I'd like to bring her by, but you might run her off."

She laughed. "I'm not that bad."

"Goodnight you two," I walked out the front door.

"Be coming back," Dad called out to me.

Joi and I were moseying along inside the Glendale Mall when Crystal approached us.

"Ah ha. I knew it was another woman. I should have known it was you who caused my man to stray!" Crystal shouted as she charged at Joi like a bull.

"Crystal, don't cause a scene," I said.

"How has Randy been?" Crystal asked Joi. "Curtis, Randy told me that you took his girlfriend, but he wouldn't tell me the witch's name. This explains it!" Crystal spouted.

"I'm not a witch. If you weren't making Curtis happy you have no one to blame except yourself," Joi told her.

"Shut up you," she pointed her finger in Joi's face.

"Don't invade my space, and move your God damn finger out my face. It's gonna be on like the twilight zone in a minute," Joi told her through gritted teeth.

She backed up. "What do you have that I don't huh? Why is Randy crying over you? What's in the bowl witch?" Crystal taunted Joi out of jealousy.

"I'm a better woman than you, that's what."

"Oh no you're not," she screeched.

"I beg to defer," Joi said in a calm tone of voice.

"You might have him mentally, but I've had him physically," she laughed.

"It must not have been that good," Joi told her.

"I had him screaming my name. Why are you starving him sexually? I can't believe you left me for a woman you're not even screwing. Randy told me about that too," she smirked.

"Crystal it's over between us. Leave us alone," I told her.

Joi whispered in my ear, "She has a gun."

"What did you whisper to him?" she shouted.

Silence was our response.

"Oh, you two are keeping secrets," she bit down on her lower lip in anger.

"Security!" I called out.

Crystal ran off and disappeared into the crowd.

"We both need to file a restraining order against Crystal. This harassment needs to be reported to the police," Joi told me.

"But I'm scheduled to sing at the fair in two hours. Let's do it afterwards," I said.

Joi nodded.

Nervousness kicked in before I performed. Fighting back jitters, I did a few breathing exercises to relax.

A spokesperson stepped up to the microphone. "We have a special treat for you this afternoon. In my opinion he's the best singer I've ever heard. Ladies and gentlemen let's welcome Curtis Cooper as he favors us with a concert," the announcer stepped off the platform.

The crowd shouted cheers and clapped as I stepped across the stage. While I was singing, "I Love Lovin' You" with an urban flavor in my voice, I felt my nervousness fly away like a bird.

Under a cloudless blue sky I sung my old hits and a couple of new songs that were soon to be released in stores. I looked for Joi's face in the audience and smiled when I saw her singing along as I performed.

After my concert I jumped down off the stage and was bombarded by fans that wanted my autograph.

An attractive white woman with brunette hair approached me with a husky cameraman following close behind. "Welcome back Curtis Cooper. You sounded so awesome. May I get an interview?" she asked.

"Yes beautiful," I replied.

"I loved your concert. You were in rare form today. The buzz is out that you have a new CD about to drop," she interviewed me on camera.

"Yes. It is self-titled *Simply Curtis Cooper*. It will be released in stores in December of 2010."

"Heard that girls? Be sure to go out and buy the *Simply Curtis Cooper* CD when it drops in December. Maybe you could use it for a stocking stuffer this Christmas or maybe you could buy it just because. His tunes are romantic as ever. I love romance," she winked an eye at me.

"Sweet," I smiled.

Joi elbowed her way through the crowd and stood near by, in the wings. Good, I like the way she respects my business, I thought. I walked over to her.

"You looked super-sexy on stage. You sounded phenomenal," Joi wrapped her arms around me.

"Thanks," I returned the hug. "Are you ready to go?"

"I suppose I am," she smiled the most beautiful Kodak moment smile.

I was proud to have her by my side. I glanced around at the game booths and food displays as we walked across the bright green grass in the summery breeze. "I love having you here with me," I smiled.

"I'm happy to be here," she looked up into my eyes.

"You look so summery in your dusty rose summer dress," I told her.

"I like your summery auburn shirt," she tugged at my collar.

"So where do we go from here?" I asked.

"Wherever we want to go," she ran ahead to my car.

Chapter 18

"So what do you like to do?" Curtis asked, resting his hands on the steering wheel.

"Um, I like to read books."

"And?"

"Do you know that I still love to write poetry?"

He laughed.

"I like to eat chocolate from time to time."

"Have you ever been to Cacao City?"

"No, I haven't."

"They have every kind of chocolate under the sun. We can go there," he leaned over and kissed me.

It felt like a magnet drew my lips to his as he passionately pressed his lips on mines. I had been thirsting for a man like Curtis. His kiss was like a fountain of water in a hot desert.

"Aw baby," he moaned. "I like the way you kiss."

"Oh Curtis," I said, lost in emotions. I suddenly pulled myself away from his loving arms as if I were resisting temptation.

"It's time for you to stop keeping me at a distance. I want to merge you sexy-nerd. When are you going to give in to me? I broke up with Crystal for you," he pressured.

"I'm sure the right time will be soon," I nodded.

"Are you sure?" he asked as if he were annoyed.

"Yes," I nodded.

He inserted his key into the ignition of his black Infinity and we headed out to Cacao City, which was a blast.

I waltzed into the kitchen humming a tune I never heard before. Suddenly, I felt creativity calling me, so I ran to grab my journal off of the coffee table and began to write a song.

The words flowed from my pen as I connected with my creative side. Anticipating the finish product, I began to sing some of the words that I had written.

Running my fingers across the page, I felt lit up inside just from looking at the words of the song. Finding the right words for a song or poem is like an artist sketching out a promising work of art in progress.

The phone rang cutting into my thoughts.

"Hello," I answered.

"Hi baby. What ya doing?" Curtis asked.

"Hi sweetie. Creativity is calling me. I was humming a tune I never heard before and then I decided to put words to the melody," I told him.

"How's it coming?"

"Slowly, but surely. I've written the first verse and the chorus. I like it. I think it might sound nice with an acoustic guitar accompaniment."

"Let's hear it."

"Alright. Here it is." I sung the song in my best singing voice.

"It sounds great. I think it's funny how you sing like a white girl and I sing like a black boy," Curtis told me.

"I'm not trying to sing that way, that's just the way my voice sounds. One thing that gets me about it, I actually have to make an effort to sing like black people sing. I listen to Joycia sometimes, she's great."

"There's nothing wrong with your sound. I like the song. I have a friend in the music industry who can hook you up with a guitar accompaniment track for your song."

"Oh wow. I'd love that. I've named the song, "Love So Sweet." Song, song can't go wrong. I'll try to finish writing it tonight."

"It may turn out to be an air-worthy song," his voice smiled.

"What does air-worthy mean?"

"It's when a song is good enough to be played on the radio. Maybe you could get a record deal for a single," he said with a hopeful tone of voice.

"I really don't want to go public with it."

"Don't be afraid to share your gifts," he told me. "It's a beautiful song." Curtis believed I had written a song that was good enough to be recorded.

"Thanks."

It's one thing to pretend to not be shy to get a man, but it's another thing to try and pretend to be bold while performing in front of millions of people. I don't know if I could pull it off, I thought.

"How would you like to go jogging with me tomorrow morning?" he asked.

"Sure," I replied.

* * *

"Rise and shine," Curtis's voice smiled over the phone.

"Do you have any idea what time it is?" I squinted at the alarm clock. "It's four o'clock in the morning. Chickens don't get up this early."

"I know that," he chuckled. "We need to make it happen. We need to . . ."

I hung the phone up while he was in mid-sentence and snuggled back down comfortably under the cover.

The phone rung again. "Hello," I answered.

"I know you didn't hang up on me."

Laughing through a yawn, I said, "Oops."

"Joi, I need you to be my jogging partner. You said you'd come. So get up before I come over and pull you out of bed," Curtis demanded.

"Oh, all right," I told him, longing to hit the snooze button.

"That's the spirit. I'll be over to pick you up in an hour."

Walking up the park trail, I checked out Curtis in his brown t-shirt and sage cargo shorts. He even looks handsome in simple gear, I thought.

"I'm a devoted jogger," he said.

"Walking is my thing, but jogging is okay," I told him, trailing close behind.

"We can walk a bit," he slowed down.

"Let's take a water break. There's a park bench just ahead," I suggested.

"May I ask you a question?"

"Yes," I smiled at him.

"Why did you agree to come jogging with me?"

"Because I love you, I want you to know that I'll be there for you in whatever interests you have," I told him.

"I love you too. I want to be there for you as well."

I stepped off the park trail and sat down on the bench. Taking a sip of bottled water I said, "The love that I have for you is a mixture of three different kinds of love: eros, philia and agape," I began.

"What?" He sat down beside me.

"The Greek language describes love in more detail than the English language. Eros type of love is the sexual desire I have for you. Believe it or not, the sight of you turns me on, and when you touch me it makes me want you even more. I just believe there's a time and place for it."

Curtis's head was tilted a little, he seemed interested and what I had to say.

"Philia type of love," I went on, "is about friendship. I like sharing common interests with you and being supportive of what you do."

"Sounds good. Tell me more," he said.

"Last but not least, the agape love that I have for you compels me to seek your well-being like I would seek my own. Therefore, I will treat you the way I want to be treated, with kindness, respect and patience," I explained.

"I hadn't realized that love could be so multifaceted, like a beautiful diamond," Curtis said.

"When I say I love you, I mean all of the above."

"What was it now? The first was eros, the second I don't recall."

"Philia, friendship," I reminded him.

"The last was agape. I want to be treated right." He pressed his lips on mine with a firm passion and my desire for him ignited. "I want to express the feelings that I have for you through sexual intimacy. Aren't we close enough?"

"I want to know whether you have the same love for me as I have for you. My love is deeper than the ocean," I told him.

"You're just so beautiful, and I love you so much. I have all three types of love for you," he let out a frustrated breath.

"Could you be patient with me just a little while longer?" I asked.

"Your untouchable sexuality is working on my last nerve. Ah shit. Yes, I'll wait a little longer."

The sexual tension between us was crazy.

Chapter 19

"I'd like to introduce you to one of the co-owners of Intergalactic Sound Records. Joi, meet Boe Daniels," Curtis introduced.

"Nice to meet you Boe," I shook his hand.

"Likewise Joi. Curtis told me about your song. He arranged this audition for you," he smiled. "You must be making him very happy, because this is highly unusual," he smirked.

Curtis inserted the accompaniment track that he had custom made for me into the CD player.

"Let's hear it," Boe said.

Curtis pressed the play button, and I began to sing "Love So Sweet." From the expression on Boe's face I could tell he didn't hate the song. The guitar accompaniment music made me feel so professional while I auditioned.

"You have a sweet mellow sound. I like the way you delivered the song. You definitely have the look. I'd like to work with you. How would you like your name in lights and your face on the big screen?" Boe asked.

"That sounds great," I gulped with a nervous smile. I am free. Peace surrounds me. OMG! I've actually changed my career, I thought.

The music scene was Curtis's thing. Music meant a lot to him. Since I cared about Curtis, music began to mean more to me than ever. It was interesting being a part of his world.

Elated, Curtis kissed me on the lips.

"Joi, welcome to Intergalactic Sound Records," Boe smiled. "Curtis I want you to give our newest recording artist a tour of the company."

"Come on in," Curtis welcomed me in. He led the way down the immaculate art decor hall with its upscale ebony marble floors.

I mused at the rich interior of Intergalactic Sound Records.

"Here's the conference room where we hold important meetings," he opened the door for me to look inside.

"It's nicer than Health Gist National's conference room," I thought aloud.

"By the way, you can quit your day job. Right this way is our recording studio where we do some heavy duty mixing."

"Nice," I nodded.

I stood at a crossroads in my life, and I made a choice to pursue a new career direction. Following the powerful path of intuition, I felt compelled to change course. It took a lot of courage, but I did it. Intuition is a spiritual compass high above the reasoning mind. It's also a lifesaver.

Later that evening, Curtis and I walked up to my front porch and sat on the swing. Under the night sky we looked up at the stars, chatting and laughing. We thought about our lives and where we'd go from there.

*   *   *

As I walked inside the dimly lit cozy restaurant, I could sense love in the air. Spice of Life was my kind of place.

Curtis and I sat at a romantic table for two. I noticed a certain look in his eyes that evening as we had beautiful conversation over a candle lit dinner.

"You're lookin' extra sexy tonight," I stroked the rim of my wine glass and gazed into his blue, blue eyes.

"You're such a clown," he laughed.

"What?" I smiled. "I meant what I said."

"You might be a tease, but you're no temptress."

"Don't spoil the moment," I whispered.

"Alright," he smiled. "I wouldn't quit sex cold turkey for anyone but you. I'm willing to wait for a woman like you. I don't want you to run off and hide somewhere."

"That's not my thought. What makes you think I would do that to you?"

"I don't know. Sometimes I feel like I'm older than you."

"Curtis, I got my stuff together."

"I know that. I love you so much. I can let my guard down with you. I like the way you show respect for my business and me. Your feminine nostalgic ways are refreshing. You're sweet and sexy and I like that. You're what I want and need in my life. What I'm trying to say is I love having you in my world. Will you marry me?"

"I believe that dreams come true and my prayer was answered when I found a man like you. I love the way you listen with interest to feelings I share. Something's telling me it might be you. Oh, it might be you, yes I'll be your wife," I sung and rested my hand atop his.

He reached up and lightly brushed his fingertips over the curve of my cheekbone. "You're all the woman I want and need." Curtis reached into his pocket pulled out a black velvet box and opened it. He placed the extravagant multifaceted diamond ring on my finger.

I raised my hand to my mouth in awe as I gazed at the rock on my finger. Moving my chair close beside his, I threw my arms around his neck and showered him with kisses.

Curtis took me into his warm embrace, which grew tighter. "I'd marry you tonight," he told me.

Much too excited to fall asleep I rolled onto my back and stared at the ceiling in the dark, thinking about my date with Curtis and the dreamy way he proposed. I wanted to call up all my friends and tell them the good news of my engagement, but it was too late to phone anyone. I flipped on my bedside lamp, picked up my journal and made an entry.

> I could love you for a thousand
> lifetimes, a man like you.
> This is in my heart
> read between the
> lines.
> I'm inviting you,
> to share my life,
> share my life.
> Oh I,
> I want to share
> my life with you.
> No other man

in the world but you.

Curtis and I each had a spot on a TV show called *World of Music.* I waited backstage for my turn to perform. To prevent stage fright from rearing its ugly head, I pretended that the audience was made up of only family and friends. When the announcer said, "Here's someone new on the scene, the beautiful, Joi Glamier." I rushed on stage and did the best début performance that I could do. The live audience gave me a warm reception. It was exciting watching the crowd sway to my music.

After my performance Curtis wrapped his arms around my waist and said, "I'm so proud of you, about the way you've adjusted to being a songstress."

"I may be new to this, but I can do this," I nodded with self-confidence.

"You're a natural."

"Thanks. It's so surreal."

"I didn't know you had it in you."

"I've embraced your interest. I'm so happy that I can be a part of it," I kissed him.

"Are you interested in sex like I am?"

"Of course. I've come a long way from the reserved person I used to be. You've helped me grow as a person. You're bringing out the best in me," I kissed his luscious lips.

"You've made me want to be a better man."

"Iron sharpens iron," I smiled.

"Are you saying that we're birds of a feather?"

"I'm saying we're good for each other."

"This is a sweet party," I scanned the room.

"I have the best party planner in Beverly Hills," Curtis replied.

I linked my arm with Curtis's.

"Attention everyone, I have an announcement to make. I'd like to introduce you to my bride to be, Joi Glamier. She's also one of Intergalactic Sound Records' newest recording artists," Curtis kissed my hand.

The party guests applauded.

Romantic music began to play. Curtis and I began to slow dance in each other's arms.

"I love you," he whispered in my ear.

I held him even closer as we moved to the music. "I love dancing," I commented.

"You do it well," he told me.

"You lead well," I said.

"There she is, Ms. Bride to be," Chuck gestured towards me with a singsong voice.

"Hi Chuck," I smiled.

"How's it going man?" Curtis asked.

"Better, since you're back with us and your beautiful lady," he sipped his drink.

I picked up an appetizer from the waiter's platter.

"Chuck excuse me for a moment," Curtis told him.

"Check with you later man," he nodded.

"Joi, I'd like for you to meet my parents," he told me.

"Okay," I nodded.

"Joi, Joi, Joi, I saw you from across the room your appearance is like the sweetest perfume. That's a lovely peach gown you're wearing," Charles placed a hand on my waist.

"Watch it. She's spoken for," Curtis sent hands-off signals.

"Curtis, this is an old friend of mine named Charles. We used to hang out years ago. How have you been Charles?"

"You're finally ready to settle down. I wish it was me," he gazed at me.

"I wasn't ready for love before, but now I am. Charles, I wish you and your wife the best," I shook his hand.

"I wish you the same. Whoops, she's the one that got away. You're one lucky man Curtis. She's a nice girl," Charles tilted his head with a friendly smile.

"Will you excuse us?" Curtis asked.

"Sure," he replied.

"I didn't know you knew Charles," Curtis whispered to me.

"I haven't seen him in years," I replied.

"Never mind that. I want to personally introduce you to my parents," Curtis said as he led the way to them.

For some reason I felt nervous about meeting Curtis's parents.

"Mom and Dad I'd like to introduce you to my fiancé, Joi Glamier." Curtis gave a warm smile.

"Hello Mr. and Mrs. Cooper. Nice to meet you," I warmly said.

"My, Curtis has taken up with another coon. At least this one has manners," Mrs. Cooper remarked in a condescending manner as if I were not there.

"Excuse her, that's just her way. It's a pleasure to meet you Joi. Curtis has told me good things about you," Mr. Cooper made a pleasant expression.

Although I had hoped to be accepted by Curtis's folks, I couldn't let Mrs. Cooper's prejudice attitude get me down.

"Have a seat you two," Mr. Cooper gestured towards the gold upholstered couch.

Mrs. Cooper walked away without excusing herself.

"I'm sorry Joi," Curtis told me as we sat down.

I would usually let a situation like this roll off like water off a duck's back, but Mrs. Cooper really made me feel down. She had no right to try to make me feel like I'm less than I am. That was the worse prejudice experience I ever had.

"Joi," Curtis called my name.

I awoke out of a daze. "Yes."

"Are you okay?" he asked.

"That was foul. Your Mother gave me a tongue-lashing. What was up with that?"

"You're not a coon. You are my beautiful queen," he kissed me.

I pasted on a smile.

The phone rang as soon as I walked inside my home.

"Hello," I answered.

"I can't believe you," Randy snarled over the phone.

"What?"

"What happened to our agreement? We were supposed to get to know each other and become lovers."

"I apologize," I told him.

"Your apology is not keeping me warm in bed at night," he yelled.

"Randy, I can't be with both of you."

"Why not?" He sniffled.

"I had to make a choice."

"See, I thought you were a nice girl. Why were you seeing a man who was engaged anyway?"

"I haven't done anything wrong. Stop trying to make me feel guilty for nothing."

"Well Crystal and Curtis would still be together if it weren't for you. Am I right or not?"

"I see you're trying to play the blame game. If she had been handling her business right he probably wouldn't have broken up with her. The girl had issues. Believe me, there was trouble in paradise before I came along."

"So he was crying to you about how bad things were with her?" Randy probed.

"He wasn't crying to me."

"Let me ask you this, what am I supposed to do about the way I feel about you? I thought we had a chance. This whole ordeal has left me feeling inadequate. I'm not a celebrity like him. You chose him not me."

"Randy there's no reason for you to feel inadequate. I found you very desirable. Things just didn't work out between us."

"I know you wanted me," he said it as if he was trying to console himself. "I heard you're going to marry him. You should have chosen me. It should have been our engagement party," he muttered.

"Did you hear that from Crystal?"

"As a matter of fact I did. A little birdie who was at the party told her, and then she told me."

"Randy, let me go, please," I begged.

"Baby, I want you to know how much I wanted you."

"I didn't mean to hurt you. I swear."

"You better be sure you want whoever he is, because you've got him. Whatever mojo you're using, you need to watch it," he cried.

"I don't use mojo," I denied.

"Well at least I got something out of this. Crystal let me tap her ass. Curtis took you away from me, now I'm screwing his ex. It would make that redneck squirm, I'm sure. At first I thought she was my saving grace, but I still want you. She remains my sweetest revenge," he said with a sinister tone of voice.

"You're so not right." I disconnected the call.

It seems all Randy cared about was sex, nothing more. He just thought I was a challenge that he needed to conquer. I'm not going to care about him, I thought as I cried.

After the church service, I saw Gege out in the parking lot.

"Where's Curtis?" Gege smiled.

"He didn't come with me today, but guess what?"

"What?"

"I'm engaged to Curtis Cooper," I told her.

"You're engaged to him already?" She looked shocked. "I wanna know your secret," she said in a curious tone of voice.

"I had my ways. He sort of pursued me."

"Better watch out, Crystal loved her some Curtis," she warned.

"I recently had a run in with her at the mall. She was talking a bunch of BS. Now she's messing with my old boyfriend. I may be good natured, but I will cut her," I told her.

"That stank ass bitch got someone you were with? Did yall trade or something?"

"Randy, my old boyfriend, thinks that Curtis took me away from him. So he claims he's getting back at me through Crystal."

"Girl, this is some juicy shit, sounds better than the soaps."

"This is real life though. Randy and I had feelings for each other, but I had to let him go."

"Well, I've got to go. I wish you all the love in the world. I'm still skittish about getting involve with someone else, you know," Gege confided.

"You never want to be too hasty."

"I know that's right. Let me know when you're going to have the wedding, I want to come."

"As soon as we set a date, I'll let you know."

Chapter 20

"How about the two of us getting hitched in 2011?" Curtis suggested.

"What time of the year do you think is best?" I asked.

"January?"

"So we'll marry when the year is new, always loving kind and true."

"What?"

"It's a verse from a poem," I answered.

"What about February?"

"When February birds do mate, you may wed nor dread your fate," I quoted.

"Let's go with January," he told me.

"What do you think about us having our wedding on Martin Luther King Day? His dream was racial harmony."

"Yes. Let's do that," he nodded.

"I think it's the 17th or the 18th."

"Sounds good," he nodded.

*   *   *

With the memory of Curtis's proposal for my hand in marriage on my mind, I went window-shopping outside of a few bridal shops that afternoon. When I spotted a wedding gown that really caught my attention I walked inside of one of the establishments.

"Are you getting married?" the sales person asked.

"Yes," I smiled brightly.

"I can see love's glow all over your beautiful face," the petite oriental lady smiled.

Gesturing towards the radiantly designed fitted white gown that was displayed in the bridal shop window, I asked, "I think that one is just adorable; may I try it on?"

"That's the last one. Hopefully it fits." She carefully removed the dress from off the mannequin and handed it to me.

I stepped inside the dressing room to try on the exquisite gown. "Perfect fit," I told myself as I posed in front of the mirror. A warm glow spread through me as I daydreamed of moments of love to come. Stepping out of the fitting room I asked, "What do you think?" I twirled around to model the gown.

"It looks like your wedding dress," she said with a strong accent.

"I think you're right," I smiled approvingly.

"Today is a sale. Half off," she walked to the register.

"This is my lucky day," I enthusiastically said.

"Yes. You're funny," she laughed.

"I want to charge it."

"All right," she happily processed the transaction.

The traffic was hectic on the way home, but it didn't bother me a bit. I had the feeling that Curtis loved me, and as far as I was concerned it was such a lovely day. Life is mine. Love, be with me eternally.

*   *   *

At the close of the day, Mom and I sat down together on my front porch swing.

"So you think he's the one huh?" Mom asked.

"Yes," I nodded. "I feel peace of heart about it. I don't feel uneasy about marrying him. I think we're good for each other," I told her.

"That's a good sign. My baby is getting married," she said with glee.

"Yes I am. It feels right to be with him. But his Mom is a racist. If I didn't love him so much I'd forget the whole thing. I'll ignore it, because I'm going to marry him not his Mother."

"I didn't get along with my mother-in-law either, but your Father and I still made it didn't we?"

"Yes you did. In fact you've been an inspiration."

"Both parties must give their all to make it work. Do you communicate well with each other?" she asked.

"I think so. We have discussions."

"Celebrity marriages rarely last these days; there are so many distractions in the jet set lifestyle."

"But true love endures the test. I'll do my best to make it work. I'm sure Curtis will do the same."

"Keep the lines of communication open and you two should be fine. If anyone deserves marital happiness it's you."

"Curtis's happiness means as much to me as my own. I want us to be happy," a tear dropped from my eye.

"You'll be happy," Mom pat me on the thigh.

"You think so?"

"I know it," she reassured me.

"You've made me happy. I saw you perform on *World of Music* the other day, and I was so proud of you."

"I'm finding my place in this world," I smiled.

"Yes you are," she placed her arm around my shoulders.

A week before the wedding, I hired a hauling company to help me move to Curtis's. Feeling a little sentimental, I said goodbye to my old place in Valley Village, and set my sights for Beverly Hills. Curtis was glad that I was finally moving in with him. We were both excited.

"You have a nice place," I glanced around the high ceiling spacious living room.

He smiled brightly.

The movers placed most of my boxes in the living room. I helped unload a few of my belongings that weren't too heavy to carry.

"Baby be careful. Isn't that why you hired the movers?" Curtis asked.

"I'm using the dolly sweetie. It's okay," I reassured him.

When the movers unloaded the last few things off the truck, Curtis said, "I'm glad that's over. I have some wine coolers in the fridge," he offered.

"That's just what I need right now," I wiped my forehead with a handkerchief.

"Make yourself at home. Here's an ice cold lemon wine cooler just for you."

"Thanks."

"Now we can get busy," Curtis did a few pelvic thrusts at me.

"Curtis there's something I need to tell you. Let's sit down in the dining room."

"Joi, what is it? You're sort of scaring me."

We both sat on a couple of brown velvet armchairs.

Pausing for a moment, I looked away from his angelic face.

"Tell me," he demanded.

"I'm a virgin. I was going to use a vaginal dilator so our first time wouldn't be uncomfortable," I confessed.

"I haven't had sex with a virgin before. Don't use the dilator. I want to physically break you in."

"All right," I nodded.

"Why are you still a virgin?" He looked puzzled.

"I used to go to youth retreats when I was younger. At one of the meetings I went to, a motivational speaker talked about the dangers of premarital sex and invited us to make a pledge to wait till marriage to have sex. I decided to make the pledge. He gave each of us a cute ring to wear as a reminder."

"What dangers?"

"Sexually transmittable diseases, unwanted pregnancies, depression etcetera," I explained. "He also told us that at that time in our lives education should be our main focus, not sex."

"But what if you never found a man you wanted to marry?"

"I always believed I'd find the right guy someday. God always leaves a ram in the bush."

Curtis made a standoffish expression. "Ram in the bush?" he parroted.

"It's metaphoric. I knew you would act like this."

"Like what? Joi, I didn't make a pledge to not have premarital sex. I'm wondering why you want me," he explained.

"I realize that people aren't perfect. As I've told you, I love you. I accept you as you are."

"I love you too, and I accept you as you are. I haven't had sex since I broke up with Crystal, so I've been waiting for you."

"That means a lot to me," I nodded.

We had mental, social, religious and emotional compatibility. And best of all we were in love.

Since Destiny was my next closest friend, I chose her to be my maid of honor. She got together with some of my other friends and threw me a bridal shower.

As the bride-to-be, I received lingerie, pampering products, and other such gifts. The sexual toy that Gege gave me stood out from all the other gifts. We all got a good laugh out of it. We also played trivial bridal games and had brunch. It was fun.

Curtis told me that he opted to have a bachelor party centered on sports. He and his friends went out and played a game of baseball and had a barbeque.

I'm glad he wanted to behave. Promising marriages have been ruined at stripper centered bachelor parties. A lot of times, those type of parties end up turning into philandering drunken brawls. Naw, be true.

The Wedding Planner I hired made sure I had a romantic storybook wedding.

Curtis Cooper stood at the wedding alter, wearing a white suit. He looked up and watched as my Father escorted me down the aisle to stand by his side. I held his gaze in my exquisite white gown. My hair was elegantly styled in a cascading updo. I used to dream of walking down the aisle in queenly beauty. Tears rolled down my cheeks as I joined Curtis and stood before the minister. I cut a quick glance at Curtis and smiled through my tears.

We committed our lives to each other saying promises of love. Our lives were joined together into one union in marriage.

"In the witness of your family and friends I now pronounce you husband and wife. You may now kiss the bride," the minister said.

He took me into his warm embrace, pressed his sexy lips passionately on mines and lingered; I began to tremble in his arms. We held each other close for a moment; I could feel his heart pounding next to mine.

Although two lives were joined together as one, it did not mean that one or the other's identity would be lost. Leaving old lives behind we entered into a new life of sharing space together, yet leaving room for each other's individuality.

The wedding reception was amazing even though Curtis's Mom was a no-show. The atmosphere was warm and easygoing.

"You have found yourself a good woman," Curtis's Father said to him.

"I've found myself a good man," I told his Father.

"Dad I want you to tell Mom this was the last straw. Why couldn't she have come to my wedding?" A tear rolled down his cheek.

"It's okay," I told him. "Our day is still special," I kissed him.

He cracked a smile.

"She's right," Curtis's Dad told him. "I'm gonna head over to the appetizers."

"See ya Dad."

I took Curtis by the hand and led the way to my parents.

"My baby girl is married," Mom blotted her eyes with a handkerchief.

"Do the right thing by her," Dad told Curtis with a stern expression on his face.

"She's in good hands," he smiled.

Dad smiled and shook Curtis's hand.

"I have a surprise for you," I whispered in Curtis's ear. "Strike up the music," I called out.

The accompaniment track music began to play and I sung, Joycia's song, "The One You Love."

"You sound incredible," Curtis mouthed the words as I sang. He clapped his hands and swayed to the music.

The wedding guests applauded after my performance.

"You have a beautiful bride man," Jarard, Curtis's best man said.

"Yeah, and she's all mine," he placed his arm around my shoulders.

"Do you have a sister?" Jarard asked me.

"Leave her alone Jarard," Curtis replied.

"Okay man. I'll give you two some space. I see exactly what you see in her, she's sweet," he eyed me as he walked away.

"You have some interesting friends," I commented.

"Jarard is a character," Curtis chuckled.

Remembering what happened with Tiffany, I realized how some so-called friends are. At first they're interested in jumping in every aspect of your relationship and once you've told them all about your love life, they end up wanting your man.

The large, well-wisher glass bowl that was displayed on the reception table was filled with note cards. Wedding guests wrote wishful blessings for my groom and me.

We're married now, no more holding back my emotions for him. I love my Curtis. I'm going to make this a wedding night to remember, I thought. I slipped into my costume to do a little role-playing. It was a white, apron cut, baby-doll honeymoon costume with a ribbon tie and a bridal veil. I decided not to wear the thong, so my baby would have easy access.

From the bathroom I made my entrance into our bedroom, looking like a sensual fantasy. Curtis walked towards me looking hotter than a sexy centerfold, wearing blue satin shorts. A magnetic pull happened between us.

Curtis stared intently at me. "I've been waiting for the moment when the two of us could be alone like this." He moved closer to me and touched my perky breasts with his masculine hands.

I stood there not knowing what to say, and then I remembered . . . Looking at him with a flirtatious expression on my face, I said, "I promised I'd make it worth the wait." Pressing my body close to his, I raised my right leg and rested my inner thigh on his hip as he penetrated me. He was careful, considerate and gentle. I licked his adorable face, and then I whispered something seductive in his ear. I ran my fingers through his blond hair as he made love to me. Waves of emotions swept over me like a tidal wave. Sweet sensual desire flowed from my body to his, and all I could do was love and be loved by him. For I was his and he was mine. It was better than my most vivid fantasy. I enjoyed the intimate sound of every moan.

"I need you. I love you. All I want is you," he muttered.

"I love you too," I whispered in his ear.

It was sensual heaven. We made love all night long.

My defloration was a physical and spiritual experience. My hymen was opened by a worthy subject. The pain was mixed with sensations of pleasure. The natural sexual desire between a man and a woman is euphoric, especially when it's consummated. To love is to live.

> When you touch me,
> I feel as though time stands still.
> When you touch me,
> your love overwhelms me.
> You are all I see.
> When you touch me,
> the quintessence of my desire is fulfilled.

Curtis and I made a mutual decision to spend our honeymoon in London, England. While I was researching things to do and see in London, I looked for attractions that appeared to be romantic in nature.

I made sure our passports were in order. We made airline reservations beforehand, which made things go a lot smoother. Then, we were off, flying the friendly skies to London.

When the aircraft landed I was overjoyed to be on solid ground again. As we walked down the steps of the plane, I noticed that the air was a bit chilly. I looked up in the sky at the overcast day. The atmosphere in London seemed different than southern California, but I liked it. There were crowds of people rushing to and fro, with places to go and things to do, just like us. Curtis seemed excited about our trip, I could tell by his smile.

We caught a Taxi to the infamous Meritz Hotel. The room we selected had a private balcony and a fireplace. Receiving the room service really catered to my romantic side.

Curtis and I were elated by the presence of each other. Whenever we got that loving, steaming feeling we did whatever came to mind in our honeymoon suite.

Later that evening we dined at a fine restaurant that was located across the street.

The following day we explored the many sites and landmarks in London. We took so many pictures. I'll treasure those photos for years to come.

Later that week Curtis and I took a train to a lovely sandy beach near London. It didn't have many attractions, except a small cafe near by.

"This is the life," he told me.

"Oh yeah," I smiled as we headed for the small cafe.

Our honeymoon in London was a romantic adventure.

Chapter 21

Underneath the clear sky a refreshing breeze blew through the window as I looked outside.

"Joi," Curtis tapped me on the shoulder.

Turning around, I stood face to face with him.

"What are you doing?"

"I was admiring nature. You know, plants, flowers and trees. I had a garden at my old place. Would you mind if I plant a small garden outback?" I asked.

"Go right ahead."

"There's something special about spring. That's when nature comes to life again."

"Life is beautiful and you are beautiful," he told me.

"May our love remain like the season of spring, alive and beautiful," cradling his face in my hands, I kissed him on the lips.

"That was very poetic of you," he kissed me with intense passion, and we ran to our bedroom and made love.

*   *   *

Having a taste for some homemade buttermilk bread, I went to the local grocers to buy the ingredients needed. The bread recipe had been in my family for years. I love the aroma of fresh baked bread.

While standing in the checkout line I noticed my face on the front cover of two magazines. On one of the magazine covers I was kissing Curtis. There was a headshot of me on the other magazine cover. Scanning through the magazines, I decided to purchase them.

"You look like her," the cashier pointed at the picture of me on the magazine.

"I get that a lot," I smiled with an inward giggle.

"I think you look a little better than her," he stared at me while he scanned my groceries.

"Thank you," I paid for my groceries and was on my way.

I found it quite amusing whenever people didn't recognize me. Privacy, stay with me.

> Love you, love you.
> No one above you.
> You, you beautiful you.
> The whole world, love you.
>
> No one else but you.
> No one else but you.
> No one else but you.
> No one else but you.

*   *   *

"So how are things going other than the fact your song is topping the charts?" Gege asked over the phone.

"Things are good."

"How's married life?"

"He's got me singing," I said in a singsong tone of voice. "The sex is phenomenal. I know my baby is not heterophobic, he likes women. Curtis told me that he didn't know what some men see in other men. So I got the right one baby."

"White boy can bone, huh? So you've got it like that. I don't think I've ever loved the right man. Why can't I love someone who's right for me, just once? I think I must have missed something on this winding road of life. Maybe I made a left, when I should have made a right. I think I've missed my true soul mate," she choked up.

"But Gege we live in a world where dreams actually come true. I believe there is a special someone somewhere out there for each person. You must stop looking behind, and start looking forward," I consoled with tears in my eyes.

"Brent left me so fucked up."

"It's time for you to take back the power."

"I know that's right."

"All we have is today, but it sounds like you're stuck in the pain of the past. There are some situations where all you can do is let go and move on. Maybe you should go to a Psychiatrist or something."

"I think I will. I've met a cute guy named Marco; I think he might be nice, but I'm not sure. I'm scared to open up to him."

"If life is granting you another chance to love and be loved, embrace it. My best advice for you is don't give up your cookie too easy. Get to know each other. Be feminine. You know, girl power stuff. Make him think you're special. Never be bitchy to him. See how things turn out. That's my secret. Yes, you can write that down."

"Girl, I just picked up my pencil."

"Gege, I's married now," I quipped.

"Shit, I'm gone do that secret," she laughed.

"Life is what you make of it. There's a brighter tomorrow that's just down the road."

"Maybe there is," she cried.

Stepping-stones

A stepping-stone to
where you
belong.
There's something better
for you.
But you've got to keep
looking up.
You've got to be
strong,
to turn
troubles into
stepping-stones.
The things you go
through, can
be a stepping-stone,

when you're looking
through the eyes
of faith.
In every situation
there's a way to
step away
from there to a
better place.
But you've got to keep
looking up.
You've got to be
strong,
to turn
troubles into
stepping-stones.
It's not forever,
it's just a season of
the soul.
You'll step into the
place in life
where you want to
be.
Don't be afraid
to believe.

Curtis sat on the living room couch watching my "Love So Sweet" music video on our larger than life widescreen TV.

"Joi you are awesome," he said aloud.

"I did do a great job, didn't I?"

"I loved the way you moved to the music. That song is hot. You have strong vocals. You are a singer. I love seeing you this way," he raved and coaxed for me to sit down beside him.

"The film crew caught some great angles," I sat down by him. "Want some popcorn?"

He grabbed a handful out the bowl and munched. "I love the way you looked. You shined," he smiled at me.

"Thanks. You look super-hot yourself."

"Music is like my heart. When I sing, it flows because the music is in me. I see a little of that in you," he told me.

"I suppose I'm better than I thought I was," I shrugged.

"The sales speak for itself."

"When we were being filmed on the night show yesterday, I felt like the stage was my home away from home. I sung "Love So Sweet," and the audience seemed thrilled with my performance. As I sang, it was like a vocal dance, moving in and out of verses. The music was my dance partner," I shared.

"You know, I'm loving you more and more. You say some of the most poetic things. Oh, that reminds me. The other day, I was looking for something that I had misplaced, and I came across your burgundy journal. I saw the beautiful poems and songs you wrote. Why didn't you tell me you were such a good writer?" Curtis asked.

"Didn't I tell you that I still loved writing poetry?"

"Yes, but you've become seasoned. You've written some good stuff," he boasted.

"I'm that good huh?" I smiled.

"Why don't you write a few songs for me? I might use one or two on my next project," Curtis suggested.

"I'll see what I can do," I nodded.

"I've been working on this song," Curtis picked up his memo pad and handed it to me. "Tell me what you think of it." He sung what he had written down.

> It feels like love to me.
> True-life fantasy.
> I finally found something real.
> I like the way you make me feel.
> I love you.
> What more can I do?
> Hey, mm.
>
> This is the way I feel.
> The way I feel.
> I, I can feel your love.
> Oh I can feel your love.
> Oh oh your love.

"I like it. Sounds spicy," I caressed his face.

"How do you get ideas, when you write?"

"First, I find a story or an experience. It could even be how I'm feeling at a certain moment, and then I write. I could write a song about what I'm doing today or about what I did yesterday," I explained.

"Well, don't let anything stop you from creating, because you're good," he gave me an encouraging smile.

Curtis believing in me gave me a good feeling. I was pleased that he wanted me to produce songs for his next project, but writing songs that people would want to listen to over and over again was no small task. Composing music is a gift you either have it or you don't. I was determined to live up to his expectations of me by producing some more air-worthy songs just for him.

The next day, I mindrushed a lot of lyrical ideas in my new red journal and began to sing some of the words, anticipating the finish product.

"How about a little role-playing?" I suggested as I stood in front of Curtis dressed in a nun's costume.

"Oh, I like this," he smiled and unzipped his pants.

"Yes, yes, yes," I put on an inviting smile. "We all know that nuns don't get none," I said.

He laughed.

"I want you to tell me why it would be to my sexual advantage to stop being a nun."

"The reason why you need to stop being a nun is you get to feel something good and hot that will thrill you as well as fulfill you."

"Ah, you're very tempting," I touched myself.

"No baby, let me touch you, or better yet, touch me here and I'll touch you there. Come closer you naughty nun."

We touched each other intimately.

I disrobed from my nun garb and revealed the erotic red lingerie underneath.

"Give it to me baby," he shouted.

"I've always wondered how it would feel, you know. Baby show me how it feels, I beg of you," I told him in my most dramatic tone of voice.

"You don't have to beg." He stripped naked.

"How would you like it?" I caressed his face.

"Sunny side up, baby!"

My desire for him heated up. I began to show an eager willingness. Curtis touched my bare skin and kissed me more, and then he made passionate love to me. The pleasure was intense. He thrilled me to my soul.

Chapter 22

While I was in the kitchen preparing pastrami sandwiches for lunch, Curtis walked in and kissed me on the neck.

"You know what turns me on, but I'd like to know what turns you on my Fantasy Queen?" Curtis massaged my shoulders.

"You," I replied.

"I meant what do you find sexually stimulating?"

"Remember the morning you had a business engagement and you left a love not on our bedroom mirror. You wrote, "When I first saw you I didn't dream I'd love you the way that I do. You've got me thinking we can make it. Have a good one." It was a simple note, but I'll cherish it forever. And the sweet love note you left on my pillow the other night really made me feel a lot more eager."

"Yes, that was some night," he smiled. "Love note, check," he scribbled on a piece of paper. "What else?"

"I like that we still go out on dates and have beautiful romantic candle-lit dinners for two. It makes me feel loved."

"Date night, check."

"I also like the way you give me those sweet unexpected compliments."

"Compliments," he wrote.

"And last but not least, I love the way you hold me in your arms when we lay down together. It feels so natural and comfortable. That type of affection let's me know you care about me."

"I've been doing things right unknowingly," he mused. "I had no idea those kind of things turned you on."

"Most women are emotionally stimulated."

"Hmm, maybe I'll understand women yet."

"You understand my needs," I smiled and caressed his arm.

Curtis and I nearly had a role-play disaster the other evening, bless his heart. I took a lemon and tried to make lemonade out of the situation.

When I heard the doorbell ring, I went to answer the door.

"Special delivery for Joi," Curtis stood there looking fine, wearing a brown delivery-guy uniform, with a box in his hands.

It seems he didn't make up a fantasy or theme in regards to his costume. At least, that's the way I'd usually do it. I realized he was trying to accommodate me, because he knew I liked role-playing; so I did a lot of improvising to encourage his initiative.

"Hmm, I wonder who it could be from," I accepted the package and jumped into character. "Is it getting hot," I fanned myself with my hand, "or is it just me?" I looked into his blue eyes.

Curtis tried to keep himself from laughing, but I stayed in character.

"Would you like to have a drink?" I bit down on my lower lip with desire and held the front door open.

"Yes, but I don't usually mix business with pleasure," he looked at his wristwatch. "I'm still on the clock," he added.

"Ah, come on," I coaxed with a flirtatious smile.

"I suppose one drink wouldn't hurt," he walked inside the house.

"I'd like to see what's in the box," I opened the package and discovered a bottle of red wine, dark chocolate and fruit flavored body candy. "Make yourself at home, sit down. I'll pour each of us a glass of red, red wine," I giggled.

He laughed.

Sipping from my glass of wine, I handed him something to drink.

He placed his drink down on the coffee table. "How would you like to unwrap me?" he eyed me seductively.

"It would be my pleasure," I told him.

It was quite an experience stripping my husband, the delivery-guy, down to his boxers.

We French-kissed and put the body flavors to good use. We made love on the living room couch.

I don't know what his expectations were that evening. Maybe all he was going to do was strip. I gave an intimate response because I wanted him to feel he could try new things with me. I appreciated his romantic effort. I'd never want him to stop trying. I'll always encourage my Curtis to bring all his good lovin' home to me.

Step 24: To keep my man, encourage his romantic initiative.

Role-playing helps me to reinvent some of the enchantment I felt when I used to date Curtis. I also like the sexual satisfaction I experience when we play that kind of love game. It's definitely a marriage strengthener, and best of all it's fun.

Sitting together on the red heart shaped love seat by the window, Curtis slid his arm around my waist and drew me closer to his side. I folded my fingers between his and rested my head on his shoulder.

"How about a flute lesson?" I asked.

"Oh Joi, I wanted to take a break from teaching music lessons," he gripped.

"All right. I'll study on my own," I sighed.

"I have a DVD about learning how to play the flute in my study, inside the desk drawer. I'll get it for you," he left the room and returned with the DVD in his hand.

"Thanks baby," I accepted the disc. "I haven't missed playing my flute much since I've married you."

He stood there and looked at me with a blank expression on his face.

I don't think Curtis was in a good mood that day. I didn't continue to bother him or start an argument. I allowed him his space, and he came around after a while.

Step 25: Be a peacemaker.

Whenever we have a disagreement, I don't start critiquing his point of view. We calmly talk it out until we reach a workable compromise. We both give in a little, although we're both stubborn. My problem solving skills have come in handy.

Whether it's sexual or verbal, when communication shuts down, the relationship shuts down. Holding a marriage together is a team effort. That's the problem with some relationships nowadays; neither party seems to be willing to bend a little to make the relationship work.

In the Garden of Eden, God made Eve to be Adam's mate, so I know that men and women are suppose to get along. Maybe all we need to do is understand.

I watched a program called *The Real Eve* on the Discovery channel, which explained that for the first time scientists can answer the where, when and how's of this mysterious woman-mother to us all. Scientists used the latest DNA reconstructions and cutting edge technology and found exactly where the human race began on Earth. It was interesting.

There are still so many unknown mysteries about life. Scientists believe in theories, but isn't that simply guessing. People live their lives based on what they believe, but that doesn't necessarily mean that what they believe is true. Some mysteries will never be known, that's a fact. Yet people never want to say they don't know. I suppose it's easier to pretend to know; the fear of the unknown gets to some people. Whether it's disbelief or Faith people just want something to hold on to. Although, it's more comforting to believe we're all a part of some divine design.

Looking at this world, it doesn't take much brainpower to know something's wrong. I'm not saying that life is just one big cruel practical joke, but all we can hope for is a wonderful life.

Sometime in April I conceived. I was happy to be barefoot and pregnant. During my pregnancy I took care of myself. I had a mild exercise routine. I ate right, took my vitamins and stayed clear of alcohol, so my baby would be born as healthy as could be.

"I was about to put the dishes in the dishwasher and you beat me to it," I told Curtis.

"Anything for my beautiful wife."

"I appreciate the way you help with the housework."

"That was nothing."

"It means something to me," I kissed him.

"Besides, you need to stay off your feet as much as possible till little cutie comes out to meet us," he rubbed my belly.

"You're so considerate. I feel like making love to you. Not anything rough."

"Alright sexy lady, step into my office," he took me by the hand and led me to our bedroom.

Most of the time I saw to the house being cleaned and kept up, but whenever Curtis would help around the house, it gave us more time with each other.

Some people say, "Little things mean lot." It's the little things that brightens someone's day, like giving a kind word, a smile, lending a helping hand, or giving an encouraging pat on the back. The small things we do help our relationship stand the test of time.

Step 26: Be faithful in the small things.

> It's the small things you do,
> that makes me fall
> in love with you,
> over and over
> and over
> again.
> It's the little things you say,
> that brightens up
> my day.
> Baby I want to tell you
> I love you.
> Oh, oh, I love you.
> Oh, yes.
> It's not in a string
> It's not in a diamond
> ring.
> It's in the simple kind
> things that your
> sweet love brings, baby.

When Laily's time came to be born, I was sitting on the couch watching TV.

"Curtis, my water broke," I called out.

"It's that time?" he screamed.

"Let's try to stay calm as possible. I'm not experiencing any contractions yet, but let's get to the hospital ASAP," I told him as he helped me to my feet.

"I'll bring your overnight kit with us."

I was relieved that I had my husband by my side when I gave birth to our baby girl on 12-16-2011. It was a blessed event.

I'll never forget the day when I first saw Laily's sweet little face. I felt so much love for her. She looked light bright almost white, with straight sandy blond hair and hazel eyes. I was overjoyed as I cradled her in my arms.

Curtis's Mom paid me an unexpected visit during my hospital stay. I was in bed, holding little Laily in my arms when she walked in.

"Curtis told me about the baby being born," she said.

I nodded, trying to be civil to her.

"She's really light skinned. I want my grandchild to have it easy in the world. From her looks she will," she told me.

"I'm a couple of shades darker than my baby, and I've done just fine in life Mrs. Cooper."

"Well, my son helped, of course," she snapped as if she were offended by what I said.

"We have a black President."

"Don't tell me about that man," she huffed. "The reason why I came by is to make amends for the baby's sake," she smirked. "I like you better than Crystal if that means anything. Besides, you've made my son happy."

For Curtis's sake I was willing to forgive her.

She broke into tears. "I know I've been a horrible Mother-in-law, and I'm sorry I didn't come to your wedding."

"Your apology would mean a lot more to Curtis than to me. He was the one who was broken up about you not showing up at the wedding. As for me, I don't worry about things I can't change," I told her.

"I want to change. I have already spoken to him. I want to be a part of your life and my Granddaughter's life. May I hold her please?" Mrs. Cooper reached out her hands for Laily.

I reluctantly handed her over, "Be careful with her."

"Oh, she's beautiful. She looks just like my sister," she cried.

"When you look around, you'll find we're all the beautiful colors of life."

"That's true," she agreed.

I knew that Curtis's Mom meant a lot to him. I wasn't about to stand in the way of bringing peace to the family.

Step 27: Be a building block not a stumbling block.

Racism is a sin against life. We are all the colors of life; no one is excluded. The content of my character defines me, not my color.

What if racism was in reverse; where darker skinned people believed that lighter skinned people were inferior. Would it be wrong then? Life changes hands sometimes. There are higher and lower lifeforms out there in different realms, but that can't be scientifically proven. Nevertheless it's true. What if God is black, wouldn't that be a hoot?

Life, is ruled by God. The only one who has the right to judge any group of people is God. People have been sinned against far too much, simply because of the color of their skin. So much innocent blood has been shed, and for what? Color is not a sin, but racism is. I know there is a God that we're all going to have to give account to one day. Life echoes like a ripple effect; racism may have originated before this world, but cursed is the one who started it.

Imagine what the world could be if more people would light the light of love and erase racism. If we'd learn to live in peace all the trouble will cease.

Chapter 23

Men are visual. They're actually wired to notice beautiful women. I'm aware of the male's plight. There's a battle of the mind raging beneath the surface. Images pop up in a guy's mind automatically. Sometimes thoughts lead to actions . . . . Just because a man is tempted doesn't mean he has to cheat. I hope that whenever Curtis is tempted by other luscious lovelies that he'll think of me, my face and my body.

Appearance is important to a man. I want Curtis to feel proud of me whenever we're out together. So, I'm making an effort to take care of myself for him. I love and care about him enough, to make myself desirable in every way possible.

Now that we've been married for three years, I'm not going to let myself go and sit around the house wearing a bathrobe, with my hair in rollers. I'm going to do my best with what I've got. I know it means a lot to him.

Step 28: Keep myself looking desirable.

I know the games some women play even when they have a good man. She'll put off her husband when he wants to have sex and then she's surprise when she finds out he's cheated on her. Having sex with your husband is a wifely duty. A man wants his woman to be a lady in public and a freak in private. It's extremely important to a man that his woman finds him sexually desirable. I always give my Curtis sweet hot sex regularly and he's never uptight, because I treat him right. I live for those romantic moments when he pursues me as his lover or confides in me as his closest friend. I also love the times we go out and do things together.

Step 29: Now that I've got him I won't deprive him of sex.

The other woman always makes a man feel accepted and nonjudged. Any woman who gets her kicks out of trying to make her man feel inadequate doesn't deserve him. Hello. When a man becomes emotionally withdrawn or despondent there's always a reason. Love him and show him respect. After all, I know what boys like. I'm holding mines down.

I stood in the doorway of Curtis's fitness room and watched as he lifted weights.

"Oou wee, baby! I love your masculine physique," I told him.

"Are you playing with me girl?"

"No, I meant every word of it," I said as I flirted with my eyes.

"I think you're a flirt," he chuckled.

"But, I only have flirts for you."

"Come here."

I walked over to him.

"So last night wasn't enough?" he smirked.

"Oh I could never get enough, Mr. Cooper," I kissed him on the chest.

"Is that right?" He stood up and grabbed me into his strong embrace. "How about some cock in coochie sex," he eagerly suggested.

"Would you like that?" I asked in my most sexy tone of voice.

"Yes. Come away with me my love," he swept me up in his arms and carried me to our bedroom.

Women, oh I know women; from nice girls to sluts they all can be trifflin'. I once was the reserved quiet type. Now I see how many female wiles I had packed inside me. Oh, it had to unfold to find my gravy, the lover of my mind body and soul.

Like peanut butter and jelly, men and women will always go good together.

"Laily, here's your peanut butter and jelly sandwich," I called out.

The sound of little footsteps filled the kitchen as she ran to me.

"Let's wash our hands before we eat, okay," I told her as I lifted her up over the sink so she could wash her hands. Then I placed her back down.

She dried her hands with a towel.

I handed her the sandwich.

"What do you say?" I asked.

"Thank you," she giggled.

"How you like it?"

"It's good," she chewed.

"Here's a cup of milk too."

"Thanks," she sipped.

She is so smart, I thought. She's only three years old.

Later that day, Laily and I watched some cartoons on TV, and I taught her a song that I wrote. I loved the way her little voice sounded when she sung.

Curtis walked into the dining room and picked her up like she was still a baby.

"Hi Popo," she smiled.

"How's my cute little princess today?" he asked.

"I'm happy," Laily said.

"I was teaching her a cute little song I wrote called, "Free," she liked it," I told him.

"Let me hear it," he smiled at her.

I began to sing . . .

Free to enjoy myself.
Free to be free.
Free to be happy.
Free to be me.

I am free, oh yeah yeah.
I am free, oh yeah yeah.
I am free, oh yeah yeah.
I am free, oh yeah yeah.

Free to be myself.
Free to be free.
Free to love someone else.
Free to be me.

Free to be you and me.

Oh oh oh, I've got to be me.

I am free, oh yeah yeah.
I am free, oh yeah yeah.
I am free, oh yeah yeah.
I am free, oh yeah yeah.

"I always imagine ukulele music in the background when I sing that song," I smiled.

"Sounds like kid stuff," he kissed Laily on the cheek and sat her back down on the couch. "What's for dinner?" he walked into the kitchen.

"We're having lasagna today."

"Yea," little Laily cheered.

Curtis and I walked hand in hand on the sand of the quiet beach and reflected about our love. It is as clear to me as yesterday, I can almost feel the warm sand between my toes even now. I had on a beautiful flowing burnt-orange peasant dress. Curtis was wearing a white button up shirt and a pair of khaki pants that he rolled up at the ankles. It was a romantic scene.

"The Family get-together was beautiful. The atmosphere was so warm and full of love. Isn't it something how well your Mom and Laily get along?" I asked.

"Yes," he nodded. "It's a miracle."

"Miracles happen everyday," I told him.

"You're like my earth-angel," he placed his arm around my shoulders. "When I look back over my love life history, I've been with women who have always wanted something from me. They always wanted me to buy them things. They were all takers. Now I've finally found a giver. In my mind, I caress all of your sweet qualities. I'm glad I didn't marry Crystal. I made the right choice. I love you more than words can say. You've given me the kind of love I don't think I deserve, but thank you just the same," Curtis told me.

"All I wanted was the right someone to love. I think you fit the bill," I looked ahead towards the sunset.

"That's all you wanted?"

"Looking at our lives now, what else could I ask for? I know where my soul is, because of you. May I call you my gravy?" I asked.

He laughed. "Why?"

"You know how gravy enhances what's already good," I smiled at him. "You've made a difference in my life too. We compliment each other."

"We do don't we?"

"Someone must have wished me love." I kissed him.

Step 30: Never forget, love is the more excellent way.

>Loving a man
>like you has
>taken over
>my soul.
>There's no
>way I could
>ever let go.
>Love rings out
>clear and
>true.
>Refreshing like
>the morning
>dew.
>There is a oneness
>in our love.
>When I look at
>the starry
>sky,
>I think of how
>you and I's
>road
>somehow found
>each others.
>I think about us.
>I think of
>you.
>You don't have to
>worry no.
>My love is true.